The Last Exit to
NORMAL

The Last Exit to
NORMAL

MICHAEL HARMON

Alfred A. Knopf

New York

THIS IS A BORZOI BOOK PUBLISHED BY ALFRED A. KNOPF

www.randomhouse.com/teens

Educators and librarians, for a variety of teaching tools, visit us at www.randomhouse.com/teachers

Library of Congress Cataloging-in-Publication Data
Harmon, Michael B.
The last exit to normal / Michael Harmon. — 1st ed.
    p.   cm.
SUMMARY: Yanked out of his city life and plunked down into a small Montana town with his father and his father's boyfriend, seventeen-year-old Ben, angry and resentful about the changed circumstances of his life, begins to notice that something is not quite right with the little boy next door and determines to do something about it.
ISBN 978-0-375-84098-2 (trade) — ISBN 978-0-375-94098-9 (lib. bdg.)
[1. Fathers and sons—Fiction. 2. Homosexuality—Fiction. 3. Interpersonal relations—Fiction. 4. Child abuse—Fiction. 5. Coming of age—Fiction. 6. Montana—Fiction.] I. Title.
PZ7.H22723Las 2008
[Fic]—dc22
2007010107

Printed in the United States of America
March 2008
10 9 8 7 6 5 4 3 2 1
First Edition

For

Sydney and Dylan

The Last Exit to
NORMAL

CHAPTER 1

$\mathcal{T}$he decoder card to the universe wasn't included in the box of cereal God gave humanity. At the ripe old age of seventeen, I'd at least figured out that no matter how hard you try to guess what happens next, you can't. Life wasn't set up that way and we don't like it, so we spend most of our time running around like a bunch of dimwits.

I got out of the minivan and a charcoal-gray cat wound its way between my calves, slinking and purring in the late-afternoon sun of Eastern Montana. The big changes blindside you. Rough Butte, Montana, was a big change, but I'd been blindsided before. The mother of all blindsides was my dad coming home one day and telling my mom and me that he was gay. That's right. He likes guys now.

That was three years or so ago. I'm not into keeping track of misery, so don't mark my words on that. Let's just say it was in my murky past. A past that included things I'd never thought would come into my skinny little punk-skater life. And believe me, having a gay dad doesn't really register in a kid's mind until you see him locking lips with another dude. I hated it, him, Edward (his boyfriend), my mother for walking out, and the world in general.

When my mom and I first found out, my parents didn't "separate" or any of those nice things that fifty percent of America's children get to go through. My parents blew apart. Short and quick and violent, the conversation in the living room ended with my mom slapping his face so hard I felt it. Probably some genetic connectivity thing. Fifteen minutes later, she was out the door with a suitcase and I was left sitting alone in the room with my new gay dad.

There was no aftermath. No quibbling parents saying how much they wanted custody, no bitter battles because they supposedly loved me so much. Hell, they didn't even use me to get at one another like most kids get to deal with.

Sometimes I hated my mom more than him. At least *he* kept me. After my mom stomped out the door and left, I looked at him for a moment. It was like I was staring at a stranger. I asked him why he decided to be gay. He told me he didn't decide to be gay. He'd known ever since he was young, he said, so I asked him why he decided to be a selfish asshole. He didn't have an answer for that. Six months after my mom decided to forget the fact that I slid from her uterus, my dad got divorce papers in the mail, postmarked from Phoenix. I never knew she liked warm climates.

I used to smoke pot and skip school and hang out with what my dad considered bad influences. Porkchop Jones and Nick Spigetti and Peach Logan, probably the best street skaters in the city of Spokane, Washington. I did it all for my dad. I took my first hit from a bong two weeks after my mom left. I got plastered at a kegger a week later, dropped a tab of acid the next month, and got busted for defacing public property three days after that. I was on a roll, and I was just getting going.

I'm a fast learner, and my downward spiral into making the world pay for its injustices settled nice and warm into my newly dysfunctional fourteen-year-old life. Not to say that I hid it. I'm not secretive in the first place, and besides that, how was I supposed to hurt my dad if he didn't know what I was doing? I told him everything right when I did it, and the sparks flew from there. Just like I wanted it.

He put us in therapy. He put me in therapy. I became a master at one-liners and dealing with shrinks who didn't seem to understand that I wasn't the one with the problem, my dad was. He talked until he was blue in the face, and four months later, Edward moved in. So much for gently easing your kid into the boiling vat of acid called life. The hardest part of everything was that Edward was, and still is, a totally cool person.

By the time I was fifteen I'd become a heavy pot smoker, having found my favorite drug of escapism. Acid freaked me out, booze made me sick, and pot was cheap if you knew the right people. Every time my dad asked me if I was high, I told him yes. Even if I wasn't.

Sometimes I think he hated me, which is good because I wanted him to hate me as much as I hated him. I wanted him to be as ashamed and embarrassed of me as I was of him. Then, one morning at two-thirty, I found myself standing on the concrete ledge of the Monroe Street Bridge. The water looked inviting. I wondered if I'd drown, or die from the impact first.

As I stood there hating the world and everything in it, headlights came along. Four guys in a pickup drove by and yelled at me to jump. Ben's life in a nutshell. I got down and walked home. I'm not good at doing what people tell me to do.

That's all in the past, though. That murky past I don't like thinking about too much. Now, a couple of years later, I've got a cat slinking between my legs in Rough Butte, Montana. This world makes no sense.

It doesn't make any sense, because I cleaned myself up. Dad and I went through almost three years of rough times, but I've got to give it to him. He stuck with me even when I didn't want him to, and things settled down a little bit. Maybe we came to terms with each other. Maybe we just got tired of it all. Maybe it was both, but we learned some things about each other, and even if we don't like some of those things, at least we know.

My dad wasn't the most selfish person in the world and I wasn't truly dedicated to self-destruction. The bridge proved that. I also learned that no matter how much you disagree with something, most times you can't change a dang thing about it, so it's no use trying. The whole business with my dad still hurts, though, and I can't help but feel that bitterness bubble up every so often.

My dad and I made a deal when I turned sixteen: I clean myself up, I get my driver's license. I did. Almost a solid year of behavioral conformity. No trouble at school, no trouble at home, no trouble anywhere. I stopped smoking dope, quit partying, became somewhat civil, got my grades up, and didn't get busted for seven months.

Then I got my license. Then I lost my license two weeks later for eluding the police. That's the nice way to say I freaked out and got myself into a high-speed chase with the cops that ended up with my dad's minivan in some guy's yard and me in handcuffs.

The deal went down like this: I went to the store to get toilet paper. A simple task, even in the Ben Campbell Book Of Simple Tasks That Don't Get You In Trouble. Ten blocks of driving. Five blocks into it, I saw Peach, Nick, and Porkchop sitting on the sidewalk. I gave them a lift to the store, and if I ever needed a decoder card to the universe, it was then.

A sign that bad things are going to happen is when three skate punks come running out of a store carrying cases of beer, with a security guard chasing them. Another bad sign is when they pile in your dad's minivan and scream at you to punch it. A sane Ben Campbell wouldn't go. He'd calmly tell them that he wasn't having anything to do with crime, and that they were welcome to exit the arena.

In moments of crisis, my job has always been to make the wrong decision. I gunned it out of the parking lot. I don't even drink beer. I didn't even really hang out with them anymore, due to me becoming an angel. Four blocks later, my senses came back and I pulled over to kick them out. That's when the police car rounded the corner behind us and turned its lights on, and that's when moment-of-crisis number two happened. Five blocks later, I'd made my dad's minivan into a crumpled lawn ornament in some guy's yard.

One week, one court appearance, and thirteen hundred dollars in car repairs later, Dad and Edward sat me down in the living room and told me we were moving to Rough Butte, Montana, to live with Edward's mother. Dad cited the "pervasive atmosphere of negative influence" that I was surrounded by as a reason, stating further that "we just don't want to see you backslide after all the gains you've made in the last year."

Let's get one thing straight. I'm a city kid, not a small-town-in-the-middle-of-nowhere kid, and Eastern Montana is about as nowhere as you can get. To top things off, small towns mean one thing: gay dudes and their boyfriends don't go over well there. Especially when the place happens to be Edward's hometown.

So we battled. I fought and cussed and told them I'd run away, but nothing worked. I pulled out every trick in the book, with no result. They'd made up their minds, and we were going. Two weeks later, we piled in the minivan and drove away.

CHAPTER 2

*T*he image I'd always had about small towns in the middle of nowhere was stereotypical: sheep running away from guys in pickups, turkey shoots, hoedowns, fat church ladies in gingham dresses, and lots of inbred kids running around bumping into things. I was wrong. They also shoot road signs for fun and have tobacco-spitting contests. When we turned off the highway and onto the blacktop leading to town, I gazed at a DEER X-ING sign with five holes in it. "You said she doesn't live on a farm?" I asked.

Edward, sitting in the passenger seat, shook his head. "A neighborhood. There's only around four hundred people in Rough Butte, though, so 'neighborhood' is more like a few streets with three hundred square miles of nothing surrounding them."

After a mostly silent ten-hour trip to Eastern Montana, we drove into Rough Butte as the early September sun lowered over my new home. An old lady sitting on the front porch gave us the evil eye. Bonnie Mae Ingerson. Edward's mother. She rocked back and forth in a wooden rocking chair just like in *The Beverly Hillbillies,* and as I looked at the stumpy varicose-veined legs showing under the hem of her dress, the charcoal-colored stray cat picked its way across the yard and rubbed against me.

Old people make me nervous because you can never tell what they're thinking and it looks like their skin is going to slide right off their bones. Edward had told me stories about Bonnie Mae. Funny and endearing things about country life that sent cold chills up my spine. I half expected her to morph into some sort of countrified demon and spit lemonade-flavored battery acid in our eyes. Dad got out and smiled, giving a small wave and nod to her. She didn't move a muscle, just sat there rocking. Her face looked like chicken-fried steak. Gnarled knuckles wrapped around the ends of the rocker arms. She wore a flowered summer dress. Liver spots covered her skin. She had a rooster-clucker thing under her chin, and nothing looked nice about her.

Dad looked to Edward, raising his eyebrows. Edward shut the door, walking around to meet us. He smiled at me and in a low voice said, "Just don't make any sudden moves and you'll be fine."

Thanking God for my father's decision to bring me to this paradise, I walked slowly across the lawn, whispering, "She's not going to shoot us, is she?"

Edward chuckled, but under his breath. "She comes on strong at the start. Give her a few years and she'll lighten up." He smiled, then hit the first step. "Hello, Mother."

That sunbaked face cracked, the clucker thing waggling when she spoke. She didn't talk, though. More like a bark. "You track dirt in my house and I'll strap you raw, Eddie."

Dad and I looked at each other. I mouthed *"Eddie?"* and smiled. Her voice wasn't soft and grandmotherly at all. Sharp and high, and quick like a whip. Edward sighed. "Nice to see you, too, Mother. It's been twenty years, you know."

"You still funny?"

He laughed, but it was more a sigh. "Gay as the day I was born, Mother."

She snorted. "Figures. Ain't no way to get your head straight, livin' in the city."

He smiled, a lifelong conflict erupting in the first two minutes we were there. "You sent me there, remember?"

Her mouth cracked and her voice whipped. "Don't sass me, boy."

Edward rolled his eyes, then gestured to us. "This is Paul and his son, Ben, and obviously we're here."

She swung those beady, deep-set eyes my way. "So you're the one can't keep his nose outta trouble." She looked me up and down, taking in everything from the spikes on my head to the tattoo peeking from my sleeve to the piercings in my ears. "Figures. You look like a bad taste of something got ahold of you."

Dad, the master of ignoring everything, smiled and held his hand out. "Hello, Bonnie Mae. It's nice to meet you."

She looked at his hand like it was some kind of foreign object. "Well, Mr. Paul, I don't know how city folk do things, but you call me Bonnie Mae again and I'll have a piece of your hide, too. Don't care how old

9

you are. It's Miss Mae if it's anything at all." She narrowed her eyes at him. "You one of those funny guys like Eddie?"

My father smiled, taking his hand back before she bit it off. "We are together, ma'am."

She sniffed. "Funny people all over the place now. Look normal enough, though." She looked at me. "You funny?"

"You mean funny like a homosexshul or funny like a comedian?"

She studied me. "Got a mouth on you, too, I see. That's gonna change."

I shrugged, and Edward came to my rescue. "We'll just get our things unpacked. Why don't you go lie down for a while until we're settled?"

"Suppose if I wanted to lie down, I'd be doing it. Fine right here, and I don't need my boy telling me what to do." Then she got up. "Go about your business. I'm lying down for a while."

We walked back to the car. I watched her go in the house. "No wonder you're so screwed up, Eddie," I said.

He rubbed his stomach. "She does have a way about her. And if you call me Eddie again, I'll make you eat quiche."

"Is she ever nice?"

He opened the back of the minivan, grumbling, "We'll want to search the house for weapons. She has a tendency to shoot things she doesn't like."

I looked at Dad. "Great idea, Dad, great idea."

He grabbed a bag and threw it at me. "Ben, I want you to change your shirt before she gets up."

For once in my life, I didn't argue. I'd dealt with nasty people and been put in the hospital by five jocks at school for having a gay dad. I'd learned to deal with street people and cops and security guards and bums, but Miss Mae and her chicken-fried-steak face scared me. I kept reminding myself that people around here owned arsenals of guns and they had to take target practice at something.

Edward had us pile our bags on the porch, then we took our shoes off and lugged my bags inside. The porch ran the entire front of the house, just like all the others on the street, and the house was a two-story with a steep roof. Edward said his grandfather built it in 1913.

An hour later, I'd been shown my new room upstairs and unpacked the last of my stuff. A desk in the corner was a perfect fit for my computer, and I set my stereo on the dresser. The wallpaper was a nice flowered pattern from the sixties that made me dizzy, the closet smelled like dusty farts, and the heat was stifling.

I changed my "NOT A REDNECK" T-shirt and put on a plain black one. I also put on a pair of long camo shorts to try and get in the groove of living in a state where militia people ate pigs' feet, drank beer, and played tag with AR-15s. Then I lay on the bed for a while, soaking in the misery of my new life. No air-conditioning, and the heat was already bringing on a rash.

I opened the window to catch any breeze coming through, but it was almost as stifling outside as inside. I looked out. Ten yards across a dry strip of grass, the neighbor's house opened up onto a back porch. A freshly gutted deer hung by its hind legs from the rafters of the porch awning. Flies swarmed around it, and a kid, about eleven, stood staring at it. I called down to him: "Dinner?"

He turned around, his shaved blond hair glinting in the dying sun. He looked at me for a second, then turned around and walked in his back door, the screen banging shut. I caught a whiff and closed the window, wondering whether I'd be transported back home if I tapped my heels together three times. I tried it. Nothing. Dorothy. What a bitch.

I searched the house for Momdad and Dad and found them sitting on the front porch, drinking imported beers picked up on the way through town. I slumped in the porch swing next to the rockers, took out a smoke, and lit up. Dad and I made a deal that I could smoke in front of him if I gave up weed. I hadn't had a toke in nine months, and honestly, I didn't miss it. It was all part of the "clean up your life and make something of it" deal. I exhaled, watching the breeze run through the maple trees by the curb. Edward, as usual, coughed for emphasis and waved his hand in front of his face, even though the smoke blew in the opposite direction. I nodded toward the neighbor's house: "There's a dead deer hanging from their porch awning in the back."

Edward smiled. "Blooding."

"Blooding?"

He took a swig of his beer. "When you shoot a deer, you gut it, then hang it up and drain the blood. Makes skinning easier, too."

I rolled my eyes. "They eat that crap?"

"Venison, Benjamin. And yes, they do. It can be quite good if it's cooked properly."

I shook my head. "I thought it was decoration. You know, hanging dead animals around the place to spruce it up."

Ever optimistic, my dad smiled. "See, Ben? You'll learn a ton of stuff around here. Different way of life than the city."

My dad, the teacher of wisdom, couldn't help but direct me in the ways of life and show me how to be positive about things that couldn't possibly benefit anyone. "Well, as long as they don't hang me up by the feet to drain, I'm fine with it. I like the wide-eyed dead look, anyway. What's for dinner?"

Edward shrugged. "Mom has something going in the kitchen. Why don't you go ask if you can help with anything."

"I'd rather walk through a pit of fire, thank you very much. She'll rip my head off and crap down my neck."

Dad gave me the stare that meant *Go.*

"I am seventeen now, Dad."

He looked at me. "And we're guests in her home."

I stood up, rolling my eyes. "If you hear screaming, save me." Then I walked inside, slowing as I neared the kitchen. I called around the corner, "Don't shoot!" No answer. I could hear her moving, though, and didn't hear the cock of a gun. Just pots and pans banging against each other. I looked around the corner.

Miss Mae looked at me, but she didn't really "look." Not with a normal-person look. Those eyes ripped through you like she could see to the darkest part of your soul. "Get in here and grab that," she said, pointing to a basket above the refrigerator. I reached up and took it down for her. She scooted me away with her hands, motioning to the table. I set it down as she opened the fridge. She took a pitcher out, snapped at me to get a glass down from the cupboard, then filled it halfway. "Get that ice out of the freezer." I did. She plunked ice in the glass, then turned around and handed it to me.

I took it, surprised. "Thank you, ma'am."

She nodded. "That's more like it. Sit down."

I sat. "My dad asked if I could help you with dinner . . . ma'am."

"It's called supper around here, and I told you to sit. If I wanted you to help me, I wouldn't tell you to sit. Now get me that bowl near the window."

I did, then sat in my spot. I sipped from my glass—raspberry lemonade, sweet on my tongue. No battery acid in it. She busied herself with a mixing bowl full of yellow batter, her back to me as she whipped it. I took another sip. "Is that corn bread?"

"I thought you people lived on that fast-food garbage all the time. Yes, it is."

"Edward makes it from scratch, too."

She stopped mixing for a moment, her back still to me, then started again. "You don't have a mother."

I shifted in my seat, trying to be a polite young man. "I do, but she's just not with me now."

"I don't hold account of a woman abandoning her baby."

"I don't know if you would call it abandoning, but . . ."

14

"You ain't with her, now are you?"

"Well, no, but . . ."

"Call it what you like. Boy needs a mother."

"My momdad does a better job, really. He's a good cook, and he doesn't mix colors in the wash."

She turned around, her eyes blazing. This is where laser beams shoot out and incinerate me—I knew it! She studied me, and I wasn't burned to a crisp. A half smile barely slid across her face before it disappeared like a lost puppy stuck in quicksand. She turned back to her bowl. "Get the milk."

I did.

"Eddie's always been funny that way. Like a girl with boy parts. He'd get razzed by the boys for it."

I smiled. She called it "razzed"; he called it getting the shit kicked out of him on a regular basis as a kid. "He's all right."

"No boy should be raised by two men. Puts weird ideas in your head, and from the looks of it, you already got some." She peered at my piercings, but didn't say anything more.

I shrugged. Being a good boy only lasted so long. "Better than being some inbred redneck with two teeth in his head and a corncob pipe stuck up his ass."

She glanced at me sideways, still mixing. The old-people skin under her arm waggled. "You got something against country people?"

"As long as they don't drag me behind a pickup truck, I don't."

She sniffed. "Come closer." I took a step closer. She sniffed again. "I smell tobacco smoke on you."

I shrugged.

She narrowed her eyes. "You been smoking cigarettes?" She raised her spoon to me, pointing it at my face.

"Are you going to whack me with that?"

"You answer me."

"Yes."

Her eyes sharpened; then she brought the spoon down on my knuckles. Hard. "You find yourself some manners around me, boy. It's 'Yes, ma'am' to you."

I rubbed my knuckles. They throbbed. "Ouch."

She threatened me with the spoon again, waving the thing in my face.

"Ouch, ma'am."

She nodded, then held one hand out. "Give 'em over."

I didn't move.

"Come on, right now. Give 'em."

I contemplated running; she couldn't be that fast. I dug in my pocket instead, handing my smokes to her.

"And the lighter, boy. Don't be smart on me, now."

I gave it to her. She opened them up, took one out, lit it, and inhaled, leaning against the counter.

I gaped at her. "You're smoking my cigarettes."

She frowned. "'Course I am. Don't be a rube. Haven't had one in ages because the doctor won't let me, and that old bastard Frank at the drugstore won't sell 'em to me on account of everybody in this town having their noses in my business." Then she whacked me on the head with the batter spoon hard enough for the sound to echo off the kitchen walls.

"And there'll be no cussing in this house or I'll put the strap to you."

I rubbed my head. I couldn't believe I was standing here being systematically beaten by an old lady with a wooden spoon. Even the dried gel in my spikes didn't protect me. And besides that, she'd just stolen my smokes. I looked around for another wooden spoon so I could whack her back, but gave up. "Yes, ma'am."

"Get on out of here. I'll holler when supper is ready." She turned to the bowl. I reached for my smokes on the counter and the spoon whipped out faster than lightning and cracked my knuckles again. Then she went back to mixing. "We got ourselves a deal. You get me smokes without Eddie knowing about it and I'll overlook the fact that you shouldn't be smoking in the first place. Now get."

I walked outside, rubbing my hand. Edward and Dad were still sitting on the porch, and a man was standing at the steps, talking to them. Dad gave me a look when I came out, then turned his attention back to the conversation. The man, a few years older than my dad, looked at me with dark eyes set in a gaunt, weather-beaten face. With skinny arms, legs sheathed in Wranglers, and a tight short-sleeved checked shirt and pointy-toed cowboy boots, he had a pooch over his belt buckle and carefully combed salt-and-pepper hair. Tension oozed from him like bad B.O.

Dad introduced me. "Mr. Hinks, this is Ben, my son."

He gave me a second glance, his face a statue. No nod, no handshake, no hello. His eyes went back to Edward. "Didn't think I'd ever see you back here, Eddie."

Edward gave him a stilted smile. "Didn't really ever think I'd be back, Norman."

Mr. Hinks looked around, swiveling his head to survey the neighborhood. "Some things don't change."

Edward shrugged. "Some things do."

"Be here long?"

Edward smiled. "As long as it takes."

I'd never heard Edward talk like he was talking. Usually there was some sort of sarcastic humor in everything he said, but now he was careful. Guarded. Mr. Hinks cleared his throat. "Got me a son named Billy. You'll see him around, I'm sure."

Edward looked at Mr. Hinks's hands. No wedding ring. "Mrs. Hinks?"

Mr. Hinks smirked. "Up and left three years back. Never was right in the head."

Dad spoke up. "I'm sorry to hear that."

Mr. Hinks glanced at Dad, then turned his attention back to Edward. "You'll be wanting to leave him be."

"Who?"

"My boy. Not to be offensive about it, but you know I never held account of the way you are." He nodded when Edward remained silent. "And with us bein' neighbors and all, I thought I'd just set things straight so we can get along without no trouble."

Edward smiled, some of his sarcasm coming back. "It's not contagious, Norman. Unless you want it to be."

Mr. Hinks cleared his throat, a tinge of anger coming into his voice. "I told you I ain't giving offense here, and I don't mean no harm, but I got a boy to raise the way

I see fit, and you and I see things different. Ain't nothing else than that."

Edward took a drink of beer. "Not like the harm you meant when we were kids, right?"

Mr. Hinks shook his head. "We ain't kids no more, Eddie, and I'm not sayin' that what I did to you when we was youngsters was Christian, but I'm not going to stand here and try to make peace with my neighbor and be put on about it. You live your life and I live mine and we don't have no conflict. That's all. I got nothing against you as long as you and yours keep to yourselfs."

Dad, of course, didn't say anything. Edward, surprisingly, didn't tell Mr. Hinks where to shove it. I smiled, then sat on the steps to the side of them. "You know, I read something once where they said that guys who hate fags actually want to get it on with another dude. You know, some sort of subliminal thing."

Dad stared at me like he'd enjoy killing me, Edward sighed and took a drink of his beer, and Mr. Hinks scowled before completely ignoring me. I watched the muscles in his jaw work before he spoke to Edward. "I came over to say my hellos and I guess I've done it, and I don't need no kid mouthing me without getting put in his place for it."

Edward nodded. "I guess you have said hello, Norman. Goodbye."

After he'd gone, Edward looked at me. "Ever think of going into community relations, Benjamin? You have such a knack for diplomacy."

I smiled. "What's with him, anyway? Going for the Jerkoff of the Year award or something?"

Dad shook his head. "I don't think he was trying to start something, Ben. I think he's not used to different lifestyles, and it will just take a while for him to see that we're not a threat."

Edward smiled. "Yes, we must educate and enlighten, not intimidate and alienate." He looked at Dad. "Didn't Liberace say that? Or was it the Pope? I distinctly recollect somebody in the entertainment business saying that."

I remembered the deer hanging by its heels, then shrugged. "Well, at least he didn't alienate himself or anything. God knows we wouldn't want that."

Edward smiled. "You have batter running down your forehead."

I wiped at it. "Your mom beat me up with a wooden spoon."

Edward laughed. "Don't mouth her."

"How'd you know I mouthed her?"

He raised his beer and clinked bottles with Dad as they enjoyed some inside joke about me being abused by an old woman with cooking utensils. "Hurts, doesn't it?"

I nearly told them she stole my cigarettes, but remembered our deal. If I broke it, she'd probably sneak into my room tonight and eviscerate me with a paring knife. "What's a rube?"

"She called you a rube?"

"Yeah."

"A rube is an idiot."

I rolled my eyes. "Very funny. Supper's almost ready."

Dad looked at me. "Supper?"

"Whatever. That's how they say it around here, and you didn't just have your knuckles broken by a crazy old bag."

Dad lowered his voice. "Respect, Ben. You know . . ."

Edward laughed. "Paul, if there is one thing my mother is, it's a crazy old bag. Just don't say that around her or you'll wish for the spoon."

CHAPTER 3

*T*he first week of imprisonment at the Redneck Internment Camp for Teenage Degenerates began in my room because I didn't want to go outside and be lynched. I liked pretending it was a sauna, because if I didn't, it would be considered an oven. I wondered why the whole town, even situated in a hollow as it was, didn't shrivel up and crumble to dust in the heat. No wonder Miss Mae's face looked like a slab of dried leather. Anything would, after eighty years in this heat.

I didn't even know how long we were going to be here. Every time I asked Dad, he shrugged and told me that he didn't know. Wasn't sure. We'll see how things go. That—coming from my dad, who was the most consistent and scheduled person in the world—was one thing: bullshit. What it meant was that he didn't want to tell me, and the only reason he wouldn't want to tell me was because I'd go off the deep end if I knew. And going off the deep end meant *permanent*. Or at least until I turned eighteen and skated this joint myself.

And that meant the grim and dim possibility of school. My grand and supposed-to-be-wonderful senior year. I pictured Rough Butte High School as a one-room clapboard building with a corral instead of a parking lot. Hitch your horse to the rail, step in, and learn your numbers, boy. I'd take my lunch to school in a tin pail just like Laura Ingalls on *Little House on the Prairie.* Yahoo.

Life in Rough Butte consisted of two things: being bored and coming downstairs when Miss Mae yelled that it was time to eat. I did see the kid next door, Billy, take a dead cat by the tail, open the gate in the rear of the backyard, and disappear into the fields with it. Pure entertainment.

By the time I decided I should venture out into no-man's-land, I'd sweated at least a swimming pool. I couldn't stand it anymore, and the whopping three channels we got on the TV didn't cut it, because even if there was a show on that I liked, every time Miss Mae walked by, she grumbled and turned it off.

Miss Mae was nothing but misery. She didn't smile about anything, and I wondered if her face would fall off if she did. The last time she walked by and turned the TV off, I turned it back on before she got out of the room. Hellfire and damnation erupted in the house. She spun around quick as a cat, her eyes burning into me. "You got a problem with my television being turned off when I turn it off, Benjamin?"

"Yeah. I was watching it."

"You'll watch it when I say you'll watch it." She stomped over and turned it off.

I pushed the remote button and turned it back on. "What's the big deal? It's just TV."

She put her hands on her hips. "It ain't just television, it's a waste of time for no-accounts that waste time." Then her voice cracked through the house. "EDDIE!"

Edward, thinking she'd hurt herself or something, sprang through the front door, then stopped, relaxing when he remembered that his mom didn't have a nervous system. She couldn't be hurt. He looked from her to me and back to her. "Yes?"

She pointed a talon at the TV. "You get this infernal thing out of my house this instant! I won't have this . . . boy . . . sitting around in my house all day watching it. Out. Out right now or I'll get your father's shotgun and kill it."

Edward sighed. "Mom . . ."

She faced him, her eyes challenging. Then she grimaced, nodding her head. "So you think livin' in the city for all these years makes it just fine to sass your mother? Don't you think for a second that I can't strap a full-grown man if I've a mind to, Eddie. Get it out of my house!"

Edward stared icicles at me, like I was to blame. I shook my head. "I was just watching the damn thing."

The next thing I knew, Miss Mae's hand flashed out and I'd just been slapped across the mouth. She peered at me. "I told you I'll have no cussing in this house. Now get into your room until such a time as I talk to your father. Go."

I might be a rebel without a cause in my own mind, but I was stunned. I'd never been hit before. Not by an adult, at least. I looked at Edward in wonderment, touching my lip; then I walked up the stairs, utterly defeated by an old lady, and went to my room like a good little boy.

Dad knocked on the door a few minutes later. "Have a word, Ben?"

I turned from playing a stupid computer game. "Sure."

He sat on the bed. "You've got to understand something, Ben."

"What? That this place sucks? I understand."

"Miss Mae is strict."

"Really? Jesus, I hadn't figured that one out."

He stood up, which was totally unlike him. Usually he'd settle in for an hour-long talk. "Mind yourself around her, Ben. That's all I have to say. You can come out when you're ready." Then he left.

Ready? I was seventeen years old, and they were treating me like I was five. I grabbed my skateboard and headed downstairs. I didn't care if a punked-out city kid with tattoos, piercings, Converse All Stars, and liberty spikes on his head might cause a few stares in this burg, I had to get out. Miss Mae sat on the front porch, fanning herself. She looked at my board, then at me, like nothing had happened. "What in God's green earth is that contraption?"

"A skateboard."

"What does it do?"

I held it up. "It rolls. You ride it."

She grunted, eyeing the thing suspiciously. "I don't hold by nothing that doesn't have a steering wheel. Good way to break your fool neck, if you ask me."

"Want to try?"

She sneered. "You trying to kill me before the Lord takes me away in his own time?"

I smiled. "No. I just wanted to see you break a hip."

Even though she was still evil, her tone was lighter. "I got myself the ones I was born with and plan on keepin' 'em until I don't need 'em anymore."

I smiled. "See? Watch." I flipped the board down on the porch and jumped down the stairs, landing it perfect.

Her brow furrowed. "Do that again."

"Why?"

"Don't you question me!" she barked, then gestured with a saggy arm for me to do it again. I did, landing it like I did the first time. She nodded, then shooed me away. "Get on out of here, and stay out of trouble."

I nodded, skating down the walk. "Bye."

She called to me, her firecracker voice snapping over the street: "You be late for supper and I'll skin your behind!"

I waved and went on my way, on a mission to get more smokes. Miss Mae was like an old record, all scratchy and rough but still functional. She'd skin you, strap you, eat your liver, take you by the ears and beat some sense into your head. I'd been hit with a wooden spoon more times in the last week than I liked to think about, and even though the thought of getting slapped in the face burned hot, there was something about her that I sort of liked. She was like a rebel herself.

Rough Butte, population four hundred and sixty-three not counting several dozen chickens roaming the streets, had a stagnant creek running through it, a bunch of small stores, and huge oak and maple trees growing everywhere. A town-square park with a wishing well and a bridge over the creek sat in the middle of everything.

If I were one to admire quaint small-town life, with its clean streets, old-fashioned sidewalk lampposts and all the trimmings, Rough Butte might have been cool, but I'm not one to appreciate anything without a grind rail on it. I couldn't find a decent one in the whole rotten place. But I did find the sheriff. Actually, he found me.

There are no cars in Rough Butte. Everybody drives trucks. Most of them had rifles in the cab windows, and I figured impromptu animal-killing went on quite a bit around here. That included the sheriff. He drove a full-size K-5 Blazer, and he drove up alongside me as I skated home from the drugstore, two packs of smokes stuffed in my pockets and waterfalls of sweat streaking down my body.

He wore a real cowboy hat and had a mustache, like every other cop in the history of the world. Tall and big-shouldered, and probably about fifty years old by the lines on his face, he wore a tan uniform. He gave me the eye as I skated, then tipped his hat to me, idling his truck under the trees. "Howdy," he said.

I thought I'd been transported to a John Wayne movie. I stopped skating and made sure my hands were out of my pockets. I knew the procedure because I'd been hassled a million times back home, and if Spokane cops have one thing they're good at, it's acting like they're mini-gods instead of armed meter maids. I didn't figure it was any different here. "Hey."

He smiled a definite not-cop smile. "You the new people staying with Bonnie Mae?"

"Yes."

"From over Spokane way?"

"Yeah." I looked at him, wondering what was wrong. He was treating me like a human being, and I thought that went against cop training.

He laughed. "Likely bored out of your head, huh?"

I nodded, loosening up a bit. "And hot."

"Your name's Ben, right? Dad is Paul?"

I nodded.

He adjusted his cowboy hat. "My name is John Wilkins. I've known your . . ." He looked out the windshield, trying to find a word for "your faggot dad's faggot husband."

I looked at my feet, embarrassed for the first time in a long time about it. "Stepdad."

He nodded. "Yeah, your stepdad. I've known him ever since he was a kid. 'Course he left and all, but I knew him."

I looked at him, not buying it and angry at my shame. Edward hadn't "left." He'd been shipped off. "I take it they don't like fags around here."

He blinked, then nodded. "You don't mince words, do you?"

"I know what most people think."

"Not what all people think."

I laughed. "And now you're going to tell me when the Rough Butte Gay Day Parade is? I'd bet that's popular."

He laughed back, an open, easy one. "Not saying that, Ben. Just saying it might not be as bad as you think."

"Tell that to Mr. Hinks."

"Norman Hinks is an opinionated man, sure enough. But he's decent." He put the Blazer in drive. "You say hello to Eddie for me, huh? And keep your chin up with Miss Mae." He shook his head and smiled. "One woman in the whole state of Montana I wouldn't want to cross, that one. Tough as nails."

All in all, everything was good. He hadn't beaten me to a pulp with his nightstick, at any rate, and besides the fact that every person in town stared at me like I was some deformed retard with spiked hair and calf-length shorts, Rough Butte wasn't that bad, despite being a slab of petrified beef jerky sitting smack-dab in the middle of an inferno.

It's funny how, a block later, things can change. It's the decoder-card thing. I'd never fallen in love with a girl in work boots, and I never thought I would. I did right then, though.

If there's one weakness I have in my sarcastic and cynical little heart, it's falling in love. I'm a believer in love at first sight, and I've no control over myself. A block after the sheriff left, I saw her getting into a pickup truck and I knew I should run. I should turn away and skate to Oklahoma or Utah and join a commune. I should avert my eyes and think about nuns or dead kittens. I should think about Dad and Edward knocking boots. Impossible. When it comes to females, I'm mush.

I'd fallen in love before. Her name was Hailee Comstock, and she broke my heart like an elephant accidentally falling on a Popsicle-stick house. She'd been my first, and only, real girlfriend in Spokane, and she was awesome. Her mother was a heroin addict. She lived in a dark, dank, and dirty apartment building called the Coldstone in the worst part of town, and we'd danced among the beer bottles, used condoms, and trash of society's rejects for almost five months before she dashed my heart to the ground and moved to Portland, Oregon.

This girl, though, wasn't a Hailee Comstock. Not even close. No pierced lip, no black lipstick, no short skirts, no tattoos. Blond hair pulled in a ponytail, work gloves hanging out the back pocket of her jeans, a tight white T-shirt, and those work boots. Oh, yeah, and a body to drool over, too. She was my country-fried fantasy, and when I saw her, I could only stand there staring. I was doomed to be her slave.

She opened the door of the pickup, then looked over at me for a moment, her hand on the door as the sunlight poured down on her. As any Don Juan would do, I gave her a goofy smile and waved like a four-year-old. She smiled, got in the truck, and drove away.

CHAPTER 4

*T*he deer-hanging house next door had two occupants living in it, and I'd met Norman Hinks. I hadn't met his son, Billy, other than saying hello from my window, and over the last week I'd seen him around, but he avoided looking at me.

Billy worked. Not like chores an eleven-year-old would do. I'm talking work work. Like all-day, everyday work. He mowed with a hand mower, weeded, painted, hammered, hauled, hung laundry, watered, cleaned— you name it, he did it.

Billy Hinks was a forty-year-old redneck stuck in an eleven-year-old's body, and I couldn't get enough of watching the kid from my bedroom window. Big head, skinny neck, big buckteeth, too-small clothes, and a crazy, wild-eyed look in his eyes—he was gangly and awkward and moved like all the right parts fired in all the wrong ways. He got around, though, and there was a kind of clumsy grace in the way he did it, like he'd learned how to deal with being a spaz.

Several days earlier, I'd watched from my window as Mr. Hinks skinned, sectioned, and quartered the deer. I couldn't help but watch as he worked the knife over the carcass and explained to Billy in not-so-nice terms how to do it.

The cool part was watching Mr. Hinks saw the head off, skin it, pop the eyeballs out, get a big propane burner from the garage, and boil the meat and brains from the skull. It was like having a front-row seat to a Hannibal Lecter carnival. Three days later, he'd tacked skull and antlers to the wall above the garage, with the fourteen others hanging there like long-lost brothers welcoming another sibling to the realm of deer death.

Norman Hinks had lived next door to Miss Mae since he was born, which meant Edward and he had been neighbors. Mr. Hinks inherited the house when his mother died, and hadn't stepped a foot outside the state of Montana his entire life. He waved and said hello in a distant, dutiful way to Edward every time he saw him, but he ignored my dad and me like we didn't exist. Edward told me it was because we were out-siders. I avoided Mr. Hinks because I didn't want him to boil the brains out of my skull and tack me up on the garage wall.

Billy was another story, though. I'd watched Mr. Hinks drape a towel around Billy's neck in the backyard and shave his blond bristles down to the nubbins. When Billy flinched at getting his ear nipped with the clippers, Mr. Hinks cuffed him on the side of the head and told him to sit still. Billy sat still from then on.

After having the get-to-know-you meeting with the sheriff, I got home and Billy was raking grass clippings. At four o'clock, it was still over a hundred degrees. He wore Levi's and a long-sleeved shirt, and it struck me that cowboys and loggers and all country-type men in general didn't wear shorts. It could be two hundred degrees out, and unless you were actively swimming, you wore pants.

Billy stopped raking when I skated up to the house. Edward and Dad, as usual for two as-yet-unemployed guys, were sitting on the front porch, drinking lemonade and watching the world go by like they'd been born to this kind of living. Edward wore a straw hat, and my dad wore jeans. They were like a cross between *Mister Rogers' Neighborhood* and some cheesy country music video.

Billy's stare bugged me out. The kid had alien eyes, and that big head bobbing on his pencil neck weirded me out even more, and that's why I couldn't stop watching him. I kicked the board up, grabbed it, and looked at him: "Hi."

"I ain't supposed to talk to you."

I shrugged. " 'Ain't' isn't a word." I kept walking.

After a moment, he called to me. "I had a skateboard once, you know. Got it at a garage sale for two bucks."

I turned around. "I thought you weren't supposed to talk to me."

He looked at the handle of the rake, studying the grain of the wood like there was a secret message in it. "Just sayin'."

"Still got it?"

He shook his head. "Broke."

"What, a truck or something?"

He looked at me, his brow furrowed.

33

"That's one of the wheel parts. Underneath."

"No. The wood part."

I knew how difficult it was to break a wooden deck. You had to slam something hard enough to break bones most of the time. "You jump off the roof with it or something?"

He shook his head. "No."

Just then the screen door opened and Mr. Hinks came out. He didn't look at me; his eyes were on Billy. "I told you I don't want you talking to nobody over there, and I meant it. Now get yourself done with your chores and come inside." Then the door slammed shut.

Billy looked at me, shrugged almost like he was saying sorry, and went back to raking. I looked at the house, then at my dad, who gave me a blank look, then at Billy for a second more. He ignored me. "Bye, Billy." No answer. I walked up to the porch, set my board down, and grabbed the pitcher of lemonade, pouring myself a glass. If there was anything I liked about country living, it was the lemonade and home-cooked dinners, and Miss Mae always had plenty of both. "That was nice."

Dad looked at Billy. "He's just doing as his father tells him, Ben."

"Did Hitler have kids?"

Dad rolled his eyes. "Leave them alone, Ben."

Edward gave a wry smile. "When the voice of the Lord speaks . . ."

I cocked an eye at him. "What?"

Edward laughed. "Mr. Hinks isn't really *Mr.* Hinks. He's *Pastor* Hinks."

I looked over at their house. "That guy is a pastor?"

"Yes. Pentecostal. But he hasn't ministered for years. He's a car auctioneer now."

"Pentecostal?"

Edward nodded. "The ones who speak in tongues and believe in demon possession. Fire-and-brimstone stuff."

Dad shot Edward a glance. "Care to generalize about anything else, Edward? Not all Pentecostals are that way."

"Maybe he thinks I'm a demon," I said.

Edward took a sip. "Whatever makes you think you aren't?"

I rolled my eyes. "So the good pastor must think all work and no play for his kid is divine."

Dad, ever the optimist, nodded. "People do things differently, Ben, and as far as I'm concerned, there's nothing wrong with teaching your child a work ethic."

Edward laughed. "Come now, Paul, are you referring to your son? Why, if Ben were ever to work a full day in his life, he'd need electroshock therapy to bring him out of it."

Dad shook his head. "I think Ben could use some work."

"Oh God." I looked at Edward, who nodded agreement.

Dad smiled. "Miss Mae insisted, and I agree. Go look on the refrigerator."

I walked inside. Miss Mae gave me the stinkeye, just on general principle, when I came into the kitchen. She was so good at the stinkeye that even if you hadn't done something wrong, you felt like you did. She had an apron on and was preparing what looked like a big hunk of mushed guts on the counter. "Get that dish down."

"Do you ever say 'please'?"

She wagged a finger above the sink, ignoring me. "The one with the blue on it."

I didn't move. "Say 'please.' "

She stopped mushing the meat, then raised her eyes from the counter. "Come over here."

Even though she wasn't holding a spoon, I knew she'd do just fine with her knuckles, and I was sick of it. "No."

She took a step toward me, and we stared at each other. She set her jaw. "You've got some things to learn, boy. Now get that dish and get it now, because you don't want to make me mad."

"You're always mad."

"Woman my age has the right to be anything she wants." She slid a stepstool to the cupboard and got the dish herself. "Call your father in here."

"Why?"

She turned on me, her eyes blazing. "If I had a mind I'd take a belt to your behind and strap you until you bled." She turned around, mumbling something about me not having a mother, then hollered to my dad on the front porch.

Dad came in, and of course was oblivious to the tension humming in the air like a bass speaker. He looked at the food. "Mmm. Meat loaf, Miss Mae?"

She nodded, then gestured to me. "He ain't having any."

I looked at her. "I'm not?"

She shook her head, her eyes meeting my dad's. "I will not tolerate insolent children in this house, and I will certainly not tolerate this boy sitting at my supper table eating food that he has no business eating." She turned on me. "If you expect to be treated with courtesy and respect in this house, you'd best learn what it is to earn it."

I shook my head, smirking. She hadn't been nice since the day I got here. This joke had gone on long enough, and this was just another of her tantrums. "Okay, I'm sorry."

She ignored me, talking to Dad. "You tell your boy he's welcome to live in the woodshed until he knows what the word 'respect' means and I decide he can come back. Until then, he's not welcome in this house."

I gaped. "No way. You've got to be kidding. . . ."

She stomped up to me, her eyes coming up to my chin. "You shut your mouth this instant. You will speak when spoken to."

"Come on, I said I was sorry."

"I don't take 'sorries' from the likes of you, and a decent man has no reason to be sorry in the first place." She looked at my piercings. "And you get those things out of your face before you come back, too. Now get!"

Dad sighed. "Miss Mae . . ."

She squinted at him, her wrath close to the boiling point. "You have something to say about the way I run my house, Mr. Paul?"

He looked at her, then at me, then back at her and shook his head, the point taken. "Very well. Ben?" He gestured to the back door.

I held my hands up. "Whoa there. Dad . . ."

Then the broom hit my shoulder and Miss Mae was chasing me out the back door. I made it to the driveway and she slammed the door shut. Then she locked it.

With the smell of seasoned meat loaf and gravy coming out the screen window, my mouth watered. I sat on a rusted five-gallon barrel of oil at the entrance to the shed, trying not to die from the heat. Even at six-thirty, the shed was like a convection oven. An hour passed. Two hours passed. Darkness came. Plates clinked in the sink. Then my dad came out with two blankets and a pillow tucked under his arm.

I smirked. "You've got to be kidding me, Dad. This is ridiculous."

He stood at the entrance to the old woodshed. The mosquitoes that came with the evening were biting me. He didn't say anything.

I swatted at one of the bloodsucking things, pretending it was Miss Mae. "You're really going to make me sleep out here?"

"Yes."

"Why? Tell me one good reason why, and I will. I'll plop myself right down here and be a good little boy. I'll even wear a flannel shirt and suck on hay straw and say 'Shucky, darn it all.' "

He sighed. "See? That's why, Ben. You are disrespectful. Even if you *are* joking half the time."

"Did you get together or something and decide to make my life miserable? Like 'Get Ben' or something? Jesus, Dad, I hate it here."

He shook his head. "This is her house, and you've got to respect her. We're guests here."

"I didn't even want to come! You made me! And you want to talk about manners? She can't even say hello, and every time I do something wrong she hits me with something! She's a monster."

He leaned against the shed. "This place is different. Different than even I know, and I understand you don't like it. But the people around here are hard, Ben, and Mae is no exception. She's worked every day of her life, raised a family, and scrabbled together a way of living that doesn't have much room for leeway. She's a proud woman, and I respect that."

I took a smoke out, lit it, and took a drag. "Oh, yeah, I guess you forgot about Edward being run out of town because they don't like queers around here."

"I didn't say it was all good, Ben. But there are good things to learn here. It's all perspective."

"Bullshit. I'm done. I've tried."

He sighed. "You're missing the point, Ben. And besides that, it's been barely over a week."

Time didn't have a definition in this place, of that I was sure. Rough Butte was an infinite shit recycler, and I was caught in it. "What point?"

He cleared his throat. "The point that you can disagree about certain things people do, but to disrespect them because of it makes you less of a person. The people here are good, but they live by different standards."

"Stupid standards."

His eyes sharpened. "No, not stupid standards. Real

standards for where they are. Mae doesn't treat you with respect, because you know what? She doesn't think you deserve it. And coming from a woman who has worked from sunup to sundown for the last seventy-three years, maybe you don't deserve respect."

I bugged my eyes out. "What? Why? I didn't do anything to her, and besides that, what does a redneck old woman know about me? What does she know about what I've gone through?"

"More than you know, Ben." He sighed. "You have to earn her respect. I do, too. She sees you sleep in, eat her food, complain about being bored, and do nothing all day long, and she doesn't respect it or accept it. It's just not her way, and I understand that. It's part of the reason we came here."

I looked at him. "You're just chicken to stand up to her."

He shook his head. "No. I wouldn't have allowed this if I didn't agree."

"Yeah, right. And if you did disagree, you'd do what? Tell her no? Pack up and leave? Give me a break. She'd whack you, too, and you know it. You don't have the guts."

"You're my son, and I'm doing what I think is best for you. That's it, and if you don't understand what I'm trying to say, it's your loss."

I turned away. "Fine."

He set the pillow and blankets down, then placed a piece of paper on the pile. "Good night."

I didn't look at him. "Yeah, and you sleep good, too.

By the way, if I get eaten or something, give my stuff to the Goodwill."

After he left, I looked at the piece of paper and realized it had been on the refrigerator. A list of chores. "Great. Now I get to be Billy's twin slave." I read them: Mow, edge, water, weed the vegetable garden, paint the fence behind the garage, rebuild the half fence on the Hinkses' side, fix the mailbox, and clean out the shed. The top of the list noted that I had a week to complete everything besides rebuilding the fence. I crumpled up the list and threw it. They could rot for all I cared.

CHAPTER 5

*T*he one thing about hot days in Montana is that the nights are chilly. It's like a teeter-totter of heat and cold, and I knew I'd freeze my butt off. My stomach crawled with hunger, too. I looked around the shed and there wasn't a clear place to sleep. Then I saw the crumpled chore list. Fine. I'd clean the shed. That's all, though. She could come out here and beat me with the biggest wooden spoon in the world, but I wasn't caving in. Not to some short old woman with a nasty attitude who thought she knew everything.

An hour later, I'd cleaned half the shed up, found a candle and lit it, and set up my bed on the dirt floor. Whoopee. I'd probably get eaten by some wild animal or kidnapped by a bunch of lunatic hicks out for a midnight ballyhoo. Then I remembered the girl I'd fallen in love with earlier. She'd keep me warm.

I woke up the next morning in a puddle of sweat, and the mosquitoes had feasted on my flesh. Billy Hinks was standing at the entrance of the shed, his big eyes locked on me. As usual, he wore a long-sleeved shirt and too-short Levi's. He tilted his head, squinting at me.

I sat up. "I thought you weren't supposed to talk to me," I said.

"I ain't."

"You ain't what?"

"Talkin' to you." He pointed to the back door. "Pa told me to ask Miss Mae for her wheelbarrow. Ours got a busted handle."

I looked toward the back of the shed, saw the wheelbarrow behind a roll of chicken wire, and stood up. "Here." I threw the chicken wire aside and grabbed the wheelbarrow. "What are you doing?"

"Moving bricks."

"Building something?"

He shook his head. "Moving them."

"Why?"

He looked at me for a second, almost like he was deciding something. "Ain't none of your business."

"Secret brick-moving mission?"

He shook his head, the tiniest smile playing on his lips before it disappeared. "I gotta git. Pa don't want me talking to you."

I looked at Billy's house. No one in sight. "So what?"

He laughed. "So I don't want to get in trouble again, that's so what. Bye."

He left me scratching my head, wondering how he'd gotten in trouble. I'd been the one talking to him, and besides, he hadn't said more than two sentences to me. I stretched, raising my arms above my head and looking at the driveway. Dad's car was gone, and I remembered Edward and him talking the day before about checking out a building in town to lease. Some sort of business they were thinking of starting. I figured it would be a hit with all the gays in town.

I walked to the back porch and checked the door, but it was locked. I had to take a dump, so I walked to the front door. It was locked, too. Great. I sat down, dragged my last cigarette from the pack, and lit up. The other packs were inside. My stomach growled, so I turned on the hose and drank.

This was going to be a fantastic day. Miss Mae wasn't going to let me in. No food, no toilet paper, no money for smokes, no nothing. Fine. I stood up, headed back to the shed, and found an old towel. If I couldn't go in, I'd go out. I walked over to the garden behind the shed, dug a hole with my heel right in the middle of a bunch of potato seedlings, dropped trou, and planted my own version of nature's bountiful harvest, smiling as I grunted the last out. Never let it be said that Ben Campbell couldn't get in the country swing of things.

I un-squatted after wiping with the towel, then kicked dirt over my gift to Miss Mae. I peeked around the other side of the shed; an old Chevy pickup was sitting there. Miss Mae didn't drive anymore, and I figured it was her dead husband's. I walked around it, kicking the tires and looking inside. It was in great shape—if faded and worn a bit.

The Hinkses' house was on the other side of the yard, and a portion of the fence had come down in a windstorm a month ago or something. That's the one I had to rebuild. As I turned from the truck, I saw Billy Hinks staring at me through the space, the wheelbarrow in front of him. He'd seen me squat. I rolled my eyes, then walked over to him. "I'm locked out."

He smiled, looking to the garden-turned-outhouse. "I won't tell."

"Where's your dad?"

"Helping some guy sell cars at the auction in Cedar Hollow."

I looked at the pile of bricks. Almost all of them were broken, and the pile was big. At least four hours of work for a kid his size. "An auction, huh?"

He wiped his brow. "Yep. He makes money doing it. Talks real fast. Practices in the bathroom."

I nodded, thinking about what the kid had said earlier about talking to me. "Did you get grounded or something because I talked to you yesterday?"

He shook his head.

"Then what?"

"I gotta move these bricks."

I looked at the pile, then at the smaller pile ten feet away that he'd made. "You have to move bricks because I talked to you?"

He nodded. "Gotta get it done before he gets home, too." He bent and picked up a broken brick, throwing it in the wheelbarrow.

I realized then that there was no reason for moving those bricks other than punishment. I also knew it was my fault. I hopped the downed fence.

"What're you doing?"

I picked up a brick. "Helping."

"You can't. I'll get in trouble if he finds out."

45

"Then we'll make sure he doesn't find out."

He shook his head, his big eyes scared. "You gotta go."

I put the brick in the wheelbarrow, thinking for a second. "Okay, I'll make you a deal. I'll help you do this, and when your dad gets home I'll tell him that it was my fault you got in trouble in the first place and that you didn't want me to help, but I did anyway. It'll all be my fault, so you won't get in trouble and you won't have to do this whole thing yourself."

He looked at the pile of bricks, then wiped his forehead again. It was at least ninety degrees out already. "You sure you ain't lyin'? You'll really say that to him?"

"I promise."

He took a moment, thinking. "Okay."

So we worked. Billy Hinks didn't talk when he worked, and I found out what a big pussy I was after an hour nonstop. That I couldn't compete with an eleven-year-old boy didn't do much for my self-esteem, and I thought about what my dad had said the night before. I decided I wouldn't take a break until Billy spoke, but the sun was relentless, my head pounded, my stomach crawled with hunger, and my hands were blistered and bloody. So we continued, lugging a pile of broken bricks ten feet for absolutely no reason.

Then my angel-disguised-as-Satan came out the back door with a pitcher of lemonade and two glasses. She stood on the back porch until she could tell we saw her, put the pitcher and glasses on the little table, and went back inside without a word. Billy eyed the lemonade. I worked my hands, wincing every time I balled them into a fist. "How 'bout it? You thirsty?"

He looked at the original pile of bricks, which was half gone, then back to the lemonade. "Sure."

At the table, Billy slumped in a chair and glugged. I did, too, and the shade from Miss Mae's awning over the stones of the porch felt like a piece of cool paradise. I cupped my swollen hands around the icy glass, sighing. "Big pile of bricks."

He nodded, an ice cube bulging his freckled cheek out. "Yep."

"Your dad doesn't like us."

"Nope."

"Why?"

He shrugged, leaning back in the chair and drinking more. "Because yer goin' to hell." He kicked his legs under the chair. "He took me to the potluck last year. It's comin' up again."

I had no idea what he was talking about, but knew he didn't want to talk about us moving in. Besides, I'd heard the hell thing too many times before, and I didn't want to get into it with an eleven-year-old kid. "Was it fun?"

He nodded. "Yep. Got my face painted."

I laughed. "I've done that, too."

"I won a prize throwing beanbags, too."

"Awesome."

He nodded. "Yep. Stuffed animal. Still got it. Keep it in the secret place so it don't get thrown out."

"The secret place?"

He glanced sideways at me. "Yep."

"What's the secret place?"

He bobbed his head when he talked. Almost like a cartoon character. "Can't tell, wouldn't be secret no more if I did."

I poured more lemonade for us, thanking God for Miss Mae even though she was a monster woman, and then looked up. Mr. Hinks stood at the fence, staring at us. "Shit."

Billy looked at me. Then turned and followed my eyes over his shoulder.

I watched his face go from animated to stony. He set his glass down carefully, then stood up. I got up, too. "Wait here, okay?"

He shifted on his feet. I walked over to Mr. Hinks. "Hello, Mr. Hinks."

He looked at me. "You've got no call being around my son. You know my wishes."

I cleared my throat. "Miss Mae brought us some lemonade."

He looked at my bruised hands, then at Billy. "Come home, Billy."

I shook my head as Billy walked over. "He didn't do anything, Mr. Hinks. I was the one who talked to him yesterday, not him, and when I found out he got in trouble, I decided to help with the bricks. That's all. He didn't even want me to help him, but I didn't think it was fair."

"Don't you tell me what's fair and what's not." He turned to Billy. "You had lunch?"

Billy shook his head.

"Get on in, then. I'll be fixin' sandwiches in a minute."

As Billy ran past, Mr. Hinks cuffed him on the shoulder, pushing him toward the door. Billy almost lost his footing, his arms and legs sprawling wildly before he regained his balance. I looked at Mr. Hinks. "I told you it was me."

Mr. Hinks looked at me, then adjusted his baseball cap. "You mind your business." Then he turned and began walking to his back door.

I watched him go, an icy feeling running through me. "I was just talking to him, sir. That's all. He didn't want to talk to me. He told me he couldn't, just like you said."

Mr. Hinks called over his shoulder for me to mind my business again; then the door closed and I was left with the sun beating down on my head and my blisters stinging like a sonofabitch.

I looked at the remaining bricks, knowing Billy would have to finish moving them and knowing, too, that the crawling in my stomach didn't have to do with being hungry anymore. I hopped the fence and started loading bricks. Screw him.

Ten minutes later, Mr. Hinks came out with a half-eaten sandwich in his hand. He didn't say anything, just stood on the porch, chewing away at his lunch. I righted myself from the pile and we stared at each other for a moment, challenging each other with our stares before I bent to my work again. He could pound sand for all I cared, and if he wanted to push me around, he could come over and try. He wasn't an old lady.

He didn't, though. He stared at me as he finished his

sandwich, then took his belt off and went inside. I heard him call Billy to the back-door entry. A minute later, I heard the belt cracking against Billy's skin, and I heard Billy take it without more than a grunt every time the leather made contact. Six hits.

I quit loading the bricks and stood there for a couple of minutes, deciding what I should do. I'd messed it up again, and I realized that even if I tried to do the right thing, it just got screwed in the end.

By the time I'd hopped back over the downed fence, my hands had pretty much gone numb, but they were shaking. I was shaking. I couldn't believe he'd just done that. My brains were stewed, my legs were jelly, my shoulders killed, and not two minutes after I collapsed in the porch chair, Miss Mae came outside, carrying a plate with two huge meat loaf sandwiches and a big lump of homemade potato salad on it. She set it in front of me, poured me another glass of lemonade, and patted my shoulder.

I stared at the food. "Did you see what happened?"
"Yes."
"I was just trying to help."
She cleared her throat, and her voice, amazingly, was soft. "Stay away from that boy for his own good, Benjamin."
"Mr. Hinks is a scumbag."
She patted me again. "You come in when you're done and we'll fix your hands up. I'll tell you something then." She went inside.

CHAPTER 6

"Thanks for lunch. And the lemonade."

Miss Mae smiled, dunking my hands in some sort of country remedy that made them feel like the skin was peeling from my bones. She nodded. "Man works hard, he needs to eat."

I clenched my teeth against the pain, for some odd reason trying to live up to her calling me a man. "My dad was right."

"About what?"

I shook my head. "About a lot of stuff, I guess. I'm sorry about last night. And about everything since we got here."

She chuckled. "Don't ever apologize."

I looked at her like she was crazy. "Why?"

"Eddie's father used to tell me that a man apologizing meant he'd done something shameful. I suppose the secret's not to shame yourself in the first place."

I didn't have a reply for that. How she could make me feel so good about myself one minute, then make me feel like the biggest loser in the next, was beyond me. I had to remind myself that she was a monster, but it wasn't working. I was too exhausted, and thinking about that kid getting strapped because of what I'd done made me want to shrivel up and die. "What were you going to tell me?"

She rubbed my hands gently. "It ain't your fault Billy got in trouble. He's old enough to know his duty to his father."

"But . . ."

She shook her head. "Sometimes two rights make a wrong." She finished with my hands, gave me a towel, then dug in a drawer. She turned around and held out a pair of worn gloves.

I looked at them. "I'm not going to do the bricks. He'll get in trouble again."

She nodded. There was no twinkle in her eye, no evil sneer, no malice on her face. Just matter-of-factness. "You've got chores. I'll call you for supper."

I'd skated for hours at a time, crashed and burned a million times, and been dead-dog beat and in pain from doing it, but right then my body was on the verge of melting into the kitchen floor. I'd never been so exhausted and hot in my life. Then a weird thing happened. I *wanted* to please her, and it went against every cell in my body.

I took the gloves and walked outside. The first thing I did was dig up my lump of potato fertilizer from the garden and put it in the garbage can. Then I got on my knees and started weeding, all the fight gone from me.

Edward had taken over tending the garden, which covered what seemed half a football field. Squash, potatoes, peas, corn, a small watermelon patch, cucumbers, strawberries, raspberries, tomatoes, and a bunch of other stuff were lined up in meticulous rows and neat clumps. I spent three hours weeding and got halfway through it before Miss Mae banged out the back door and told me to get washed up. I lurched inside and slithered into the shower, letting icy water rush over me.

I came downstairs to the smell of buttered peas, buttermilk biscuits, leftover meat loaf, loads of gravy, and mashed potatoes with the skins on them. Miss Mae sat me down, brought me a plate full of food, and lathered my potatoes in sour cream and butter. Then she lathered my meat loaf in gravy. She poured me a glass of milk, then got her own plate. I watched her. "Thank you."

She sat across from me. "You worked today."

I realized I was being schooled, and didn't mind it one single bit. My aches and pains lessened, and I actually found myself in a good mood after hours of backbreaking labor in hundred-degree heat. And I was hungry. I'd never eaten as much in a single day, and I couldn't believe my stomach was growling after the lunch I'd vacuumed down. "This looks awesome."

She set her napkin on her lap, staring at me until I did, too. "Say grace."

I didn't know what she was talking about, but I didn't want to spend another night outside. "Grace."

She looked at me with a pinched mouth, the blaze in her eyes starting again; then she realized I didn't know what the hell she was talking about. She nodded. "Bless the food, Ben."

I blushed. Crap. The last time we'd said a prayer was never, and she'd nailed me again. How did she do this to me? Nobody could make me feel this way, like I was three years old. I'd never said a blessing, and she hadn't brought it up before. I folded my hands. "Dear God, thanks for all this food and everything, and thanks for the day. Amen."

She opened her eyes, then smiled. "It'll do."

I dug in. Everything tasted golden, and I wouldn't even have traded the peas for a Big Mac. For ten Big Macs. Country people knew how to eat, and who cares about clogged arteries, I was into it. The meat loaf melted in my mouth. "What time are my dad and Ed supposed to be home?"

Miss Mae wiped her mouth with her napkin. "They called and said they'd be late. Business things."

I was in heaven. Almost. I looked at her across the table. "Can I have a beer?"

She didn't look up. "Man works hard all day is entitled to a beer if he so chooses."

I stood.

"Sit down." She stood, getting me a beer from the fridge, then brought it back, her eyes twinkling as she held it. "You ain't a man yet. What do I get?"

I looked at the moisture beading on the bottle. "I'll make you a space in the shed to smoke. A chair and a little table."

She handed me the beer. "Deal."

I cracked the cap and took a swig. This wasn't high school–kid beer-drinking. No downing kegger cups or beer-bong action or getting drunk to be cool while you staggered around saying stupid shit before puking your guts out. This was relaxing, work-your-ass-off-all-day-

and-enjoy-something-cold-with-a-kick drinking. "Can I ask a question?"

She nodded.

"Who's that girl that lives down the street? In the yellow house."

Miss Mae smiled. "Kimberly Johan."

I looked at my food. "I fell in love with her yesterday."

She slid me a small smile. "Quick about things, aren't you?"

I shrugged, my tongue a bit loose with a buzz. "Can't help it. I'm a lover, not a fighter. Or a worker."

She raised her eyebrows at me, then frowned. "Her daddy ain't going to like you one bit."

I smiled. "Love conquers all."

She dismissed it. "Puppy love."

Silence followed, and we ate for a few minutes. "Can I ask another question?"

"As long as it ain't foolish like the last one."

My dad always used to tell me there weren't any stupid questions, but I guess in Montana, there are. I swallowed my embarrassment, then went on. "Did Edward get a lot of hassle when he lived here? I mean, about being gay?"

She nodded. "The Lord doesn't look too kindly on his choice, and neither do the people in Rough Butte. We're simple people, and Eddie isn't simple. That don't mean he ain't loved, though."

I let that one go, because even a fool wouldn't touch the whole "choice" thing with a ten-foot pole. If I'd learned anything about having a gay dad, it was that arguing about the choice thing was useless. You believed it or you didn't, and any time God had something to do with how people felt, He was the only one that could change their minds. "Why'd he come back if it was so bad, then?"

"He makes his own decisions. Ask him, if that's what you're after."

I looked at her. "They said they moved because of me."

She furrowed her brow.

"I mean, it just didn't make sense. Just about everything Edward ever said about this place was bad. All the stuff he went through."

She frowned. "Edward might be different, but I raised that boy."

"What does that mean?"

"It means you do right by your family even if it causes you pain."

I thought about that, and knew what she was saying. I was his family. "Then why did you send him away?"

Her face softened. Just a little bit, though; it couldn't *really* soften. "For his own sake. This place wasn't right for him."

"You understand, don't you? I mean . . . that he was born that way?"

She cleared her throat, pausing. "It's a sin."

"That's not what I'm talking about."

After another moment, her face hardened. "It's my business what I understand and don't understand. Now eat."

I took another bite of potatoes and my stomach

groaned, stuffed to the brim. "What happened to Billy's mom?"

She set her napkin on her plate, then stood. "Up and left one night about three years ago. Girl was always talking about city life."

I smiled. "Can't blame her, being with him."

She took my plate, and I was sure to thank her. If I got whacked tonight, my arm would probably drop off. She shook her head, but her eyes weren't hard. "She's a no-account for leaving her son."

"You don't like Mr. Hinks, do you?"

"Too hard on the boy, if I had an opinion."

I raised my eyebrows. " 'Too hard' coming from you must mean something."

She turned around and smiled. "Eddie must have told you some stories."

"Understatement of the year. He told me you hung him by his pants on a hook for three hours one time."

She nodded, fondly remembering the episode. "Boy needs to learn respect for his mother or she loses control. You raise boys and you'll know what I mean."

I knew Edward had a brother, long gone from Rough Butte. "Did you strap your kids like Mr. Hinks?"

"I done it myself on occasion with my boys."

"That's child abuse."

"Maybe to your way of thinking, but since what you think don't mean diddly, it don't matter."

"So you think what he did was fine?"

She shook her head and continued clearing plates. I stood and began helping her; she shooed me away. "You done your work, I'll do mine." She paused. "There's a difference between strapping a boy for good reason and strapping a boy because you're a miserable sonofabitch. No, Billy didn't deserve that strap, I don't think. Sometimes he does, though, and I ain't going to say Norman Hinks is a bad man because of it."

"You don't like him, though."

"I sure don't, but he cares for that boy the way he knows how. His daddy did the same to him."

"Well, he's wrong."

She chuckled. "At least you got an opinion on you. Now get on out of here while I finish up."

I did, and as I walked out of the kitchen, she called to me. I turned around. She kept her back to me as she did the dishes. "You make waste in my garden again and I'll whip the skin off your backside."

I was just about to say "Sorry," then stopped myself. "It'll never happen again."

CHAPTER 7

I woke up the next morning and my body wouldn't move, but I felt good. Like I'd done something. I lay there for ten minutes staring at the ceiling, willing even my pinky finger to twitch. I finally rolled out of bed. My hands were cracked, with the blisters hardened, and they hurt every time I moved them. I made my way to the bathroom, took a leak, skipped brushing my teeth on account of my hands, and made my way downstairs.

I knew I'd missed breakfast. Miss Mae had it ready at six on the dot every morning, and I'd not made it down once since we got here, settling for cold cereal most mornings. I looked at the clock on the wall, and it read ten-thirty.

Dad and Edward sat at the dining room table, poring over papers. A young woman, probably about twenty-five—pretty, and dressed in a dark blue business suit with a tight skirt—sat with them. Dad looked at me when I came in. "Ben, this is Ms. Pierce from the bank."

I nodded. "Hi. Nice to meet you."

I held out my hand to shake hers, forgetting that

it would cause me excruciating pain if I did, and Dad saw the scabbed blisters. Before I could pull it back, Dad took me by the wrist. "Oh my God, Ben, what happened?"

I tried to take my hand away, glancing at Ms. Pierce and her prettiness. "I'm fine."

Dad took my other hand, staring at the blisters. "Edward, look at this."

I squirmed, and Ms. Pierce lowered her eyes. Edward came around the table and studied my hands, concern on his face. "That has to hurt, Ben. What in God's name happened?"

Dad interrupted. "You need to see a doctor. They might get infected."

Miss Mae watched from the kitchen entry. I yanked my hands away. "I said they're fine."

"Ben . . ."

"Dad, don't worry about it, okay? I've got work today." I looked at Ms. Pierce, and she looked away.

Dad would have none of it. "You need medical attention."

Miss Mae was still standing there, and something in me wanted out. "I said I was fine. It's not like I'm a f—" I shook my head, stopping myself before the word came out. "I've got stuff to do." I walked outside, and Dad followed me.

He stood on the porch. "Ben."

I turned around. "What?"

Anger simmered in his eyes. "Why did you just do that?"

I stared at him. "Shouldn't you be back inside with her?"

He looked at me, confused. "You're mad because I was concerned about your hands? Why? Where is this coming from?"

I shook my head, frustrated. I thought about Ms. Pierce and Miss Mae and the flush of embarrassment rising in me as I'd stood there while my dad acted like some ultra-gay father fluttering around his injured son. "I told you I was fine."

"I know, but . . ."

I raised my voice, sick of talking. That's all he ever did. "Dad, let it go, huh? Jesus."

He studied me for a moment, then stuck his hands in his pockets. "I know what you were going to say in there."

"Oh, yeah? What?"

"That you weren't a fag. You'd be fine because you weren't some kind of prissy gay."

I stared at him, Ms. Pierce and Miss Mae flashing again through my mind. Had I seen pity in their eyes? Pity for what? For having a dad like that? Guilty confusion, angry and sad all at the same time, twisted my stomach. Why couldn't he leave it alone? Why couldn't he be straight? "Well, I didn't say it."

"Yes, but it was there."

I shrugged, all those bad feelings from the beginning simmering up like I didn't want them to. "So what if it was there? Not like it's news."

He glanced over his shoulder, back at the house, and

lowered his voice. "Being gay doesn't have anything to do with masculinity, son."

I remembered Ms. Pierce's face. The way she'd looked down. "Wishing you were a girl your whole life doesn't have anything to do with masculinity? Got me there, Dad."

"I don't wish to be a girl, Ben, and you know that. I enjoy being a man."

"Good. Are we done? It's a little early for one of your philosophical lessons on life and how different you are as a gay guy."

He eyed me, trying to hide his anger. "Where is this coming from?"

"Where is what coming from? You're not Mom, and I don't need you to act like it."

He narrowed his eyes, defensive. "I know that, but apparently you believe being homosexual means somehow being less of a man."

I stared at him. Fine. He wanted it, he'd get it. "What if I do think that?"

"If you do think like that, you have to answer for it."

I shook my head, rolling my eyes. Back to the same old thing. Dad does whatever he wants, Ben has to answer for it. "That, coming from you. Great advice."

Anger lit his eyes. "What does that mean?"

"It means you don't have to answer for anything."

He knitted his brow, confused. "Like what?"

I threw up my hands, frustrated and ashamed and embarrassed. "Like what?" I thought back to the arguments we'd had and counted off just a few of them. "Okay, let's see. We walk down the street with you and

Edward holding hands and I have to answer for it because everybody stares at that poor kid who must be messed up because his dad is gay. I walk in the living room to see you kissing each other and I have to answer for it because we all know it's perfectly normal to see your dad giving tongue to a guy. I have to answer for not liking my dad acting like some kind of flamer about my hands in front of Miss Mae and the bank lady." I stared at him, nodding. "I think I got it, Dad. I have to answer for everything you do, because you don't have to answer for anything. Great deal."

He frowned. "I think I behaved like a parent concerned about his child. Nothing more and nothing less, and I can't understand where this anger is coming from."

"Of course you can't understand."

"What does that mean?"

"Forget it."

"What don't I understand? That because I'm gay I can't see that you were embarrassed inside? You think that I don't know what it is to be a man? I am a man, Ben, and I'm proud of it."

"Why don't you act like it, then?"

"That's homophobic and ignorant."

"So what? It's the truth, and you just proved it inside."

"I can't believe I'm hearing this from you. After everything we've talked about and gone through, I'm standing here listening to my son say this."

I shook my head. As far as I could see, he'd done whatever he'd wanted and I'd gone through it with counselors and shrinks and teachers and cops. I smirked. "You've told me that if I look like a punker and act like a punker, people will treat me like a punker. Except for you. Oh, no, you can't treat a gay dude like a gay dude. Nope. No way. Sorry. It's *homophobic* to say you act like a woman when you act like a woman? Bullshit."

"Son, we've talked about stereotypes before, and the negative connotation is what makes it homophobic."

"It's homophobic when you embarrass me in front of people? Edward is like a walking advertisement for the gay stereotype, but you know what? He's not." I shook my head. "He laid off inside, Dad. Didn't he? He didn't sit there and push it, because he understood that this wasn't about him. It was about me, and he respected it. I told you I was fine, but you have to shove it down my throat every single fucking time. *Accept it, Ben. Paul Campbell is gay, and that means he can be the most self-ish asshole in the world, because everything is about him.*" I glared at him. "Why don't you stop hiding behind it, for once?"

His eyes flashed, and we were back in the same routine. "Let's see . . ." He counted off on his fingers. "So far it's that I'm not a man, I'm a hypocrite, I'm selfish, and I hide behind being gay. Anything more you'd like to say before I'm condemned to hell?"

I stood there for a moment, knowing I didn't want to fight about this anymore. "I'm saying that sometimes I wish my dad was just a regular dad that had a regular wife and a regular family. That's all."

Silence.

I clenched my teeth, upset because I knew I'd hurt him. "It was embarrassing. That's all."

He took a moment, staring at the driveway. "I see what you're saying."

"Do you?"

He nodded. "Yes, I do. You have every right to be upset. I behaved inappropriately toward you in there. I should have listened."

I didn't say anything for a few seconds. "I don't think you're not a man, Dad. It's just that sometimes I wish . . ."

Dad came down the stairs and raised his arm to put it around my shoulders, but stopped short. "I know what you wish, Ben, and I think if I were you, I'd wish the same thing. That's not wrong, and I don't want you to worry about it. We'll deal with it as it comes."

I thought about Ms. Pierce, and blood rushed to my cheeks. "She's pretty, you know?"

"I know. And I know it's not being homophobic to get angry about the way you are treated. The only thing I've ever asked of you is to keep trying."

I nodded, giving him a half smile. "Will do."

"I will, too."

Later that day, Miss Mae sat on one of the rockers, petting a stray cat on her lap. I plunked down in the chair beside her, half my chores done. "Crap."

She swung her arm out, quick as lightning, and cuffed me on the head. "Mouth."

I grunted, because I wasn't allowed to say "Sorry"

anymore. There was a stupid rule for everything in this stupid town, and every time you broke one, you got hit with something. "I hate this place."

She took a ten-dollar bill out of some mysterious place in her dress, completely unconcerned with what I'd said. "Run down to the drugstore and get some more smokes."

"Buy me a pack, too, and I'll go. I'm out of dough."

She nodded. "Don't be lollygagging about it."

I walked past Kimberly Johan's house with my eyes glued to it; then I noticed the truck was gone. I wanted to see her. I wanted to run up and proclaim my undying love for her. We could have little country babies named Moe and Bobchuck and Jennylou, and I could work at the paper mill and come home to dinner and whole lots of lovin' afterward. I'd even learn how to square-dance. It would give a new meaning to a hoedown.

Bummed at not seeing her, I picked up my pace, wanting to get back before it got too hot. When I got to the town square, I made a beeline for the drugstore. That's when I saw her truck parked in front of the library.

Miss Mae could wait, and I could fry on the way home.

The Rough Butte Public Library consisted of two rooms with a bunch of books in them. A Hitleresque old lady, possibly Miss Mae's evil twin, stood guard at the counter. Libraries are foreign affairs to me, and I can't really remember ever having been in one. Dad and Edward read a lot, but the main use I've had for books comes in the form of ignoring them as much as possible.

Besides the Hitler-looking woman, there was one person in the place. Kimberly Johan. I saw her right off the bat, standing in front of a row of shelves. Today she wore shorts and a baby-blue tank top, her hair still pulled back, but with sandals on instead of boots. Hitler Lady looked at me over her glasses, then smiled warmly. "Hello, young man. Is there something I can help you find?"

I was confused. Librarians were supposed to be mean and pinch-faced old maids, and people here were supposed to turn their noses up at people like me. "Uh, I just was walking by and decided to come in."

She smiled even more warmly. "You must be Benjamin Campbell. Welcome to Rough Butte."

I wondered if my name was tattooed on my forehead. I nodded. "Thank you."

"I take it you like reading? We might not have as big a selection as the city, but I think you might be able to find something here to your liking."

I glanced toward Kimberly. "Actually, I think I know what I want."

She looked at Kimberly, then smiled and gave me a wink. "Well, good luck, then. You just make yourself at home."

Kimberly had a book out and was flipping through the pages. I mustered up my best walk and sauntered down the aisle, stopping next to her and pretending to look at the shelves. She was at least five-eleven. Three inches taller than me. I could learn to love tall women.

She didn't look up from her book. "Need an attorney?"

I looked at her, wondering if she was crazy in the head. Just my luck to fall in love with a loon. "Why? Do I look like I need one?"

She rolled her eyes, her face cheery and her eyes deep blue. "Well, you are in the law section."

I looked at the books. "Oh, yeah. No, I was just . . . I've always had a fascination with the law. You know, laws and everything."

She laughed. "Your name is Ben, right?"

"This town doesn't have many secrets, does it?"

She lowered her voice conspiratorially. "Eyes and ears everywhere."

I nodded. "You're Kimberly."

She smiled. "Like I said, eyes and ears everywhere."

"I asked my Momdad's mother, Miss Mae, who you were." I looked at her. "You live down the street from us. I saw you the day before yesterday."

Her eyes widened in surprise at the Momdad comment, which told me she knew about our "circumstances," but she let it pass. "I know. I was going to my uncle's farm to help bale."

"Bail what? A boat?"

She laughed. "Hay. Bale hay."

"Oh. Those square straw things, right?"

"You *are* from the city, aren't you?"

I shrugged. "I've never eaten anything I've killed or smoked a corncob pipe, if that's what you mean."

She frowned. "Not everybody in a small town is like that, you know."

"Ouch. So that means you're not interested in a date with a city guy?"

She looked at the books, then at the carpet, then anywhere but at me. "I'm really busy."

"Have a boyfriend?"

"Not really. Just busy."

"Not really" meant "yes" in my book, but I didn't push it, because even though I might be girl-dumb, Edward had taught me that women speak a different language. "Does everybody work around here?"

She looked at me, confused. "Like how?"

I shook my head, suddenly embarrassed. "It just seems like everybody around here is always doing something."

"Not always. Just regular stuff."

I thought about her baling hay. "Like baling?"

She nodded. "Yes."

"What if we went on a baling date?"

She narrowed her eyes, looking confused. "What?"

"Well, if you won't go on a regular date with me, take me baling. I can work."

She thought about it for a moment. "My uncle can always use a hand, and it's twelve dollars an hour."

"Deal. Count me in." I smiled. "When are you going again?"

"Tonight."

Every muscle in my body ached, and my hands were shot. I could barely unzip to take a leak. "Okay. I'll come by. What time?"

"Four-thirty. When it cools down." She smiled. "You can meet my dad."

CHAPTER 8

*B*efore my first-ever date with my first-ever girlfriend, Hailee Comstock, Edward sat me down and gave me the skinny on date etiquette. Edward knew everything about fashion, manners, date planning, what to do, what to say, how to treat a woman, and what they appreciate. In fact, Ed is the closest thing to a woman I know who's not a woman.

Now the test for him would really come. An hour after I talked to Kimberly, I found him watering squash in the garden. "Hey, Edward," I said. He gave me a foul look, then squirted me with the hose. I remembered the squat I'd taken out here. "Miss Mae told you about my gift to the garden?"

He gave me a sideways glance. "You're lucky I don't relieve myself in your bed, young delinquent."

I shrugged. "Come on, Ed. It makes good fertilizer."

He threatened me with the hose. "Yes, but the spite and retribution make it stink more. And my name is Edward."

"Sorry."

He smiled. "Come to help me tend the squash, or is that a bit too feminine for you?"

I groaned, knowing Edward was talking about Ms. Pierce. Not a good situation when you wanted something. I knew I couldn't blow it off. "Dad talked to you?"

"He certainly did, and as a woman of the new millennium, I've got to say I'm deeply offended."

"Edward . . ."

He laughed. "You know it's not my style to get offended by the likes of you, Ben, so calm down. You got a little pissy about us flamers pattering about you in front of a good-looking woman in a tight skirt, and I don't blame you."

"*You* didn't do it. And I didn't mean it that way."

His smile was still there, but there was that look in his eyes where I knew he'd been upset by it. He nodded. "I know, but sometimes what it means to you isn't what it means to other people."

"I don't hate fags."

He laughed like I was the most hopeless person in the world. "'I don't hate fags.' Isn't that statement sort of oxymoronic?"

Edward liked doing those things. He could point out the truth *and* call me a moron at the same time. He could also let me know I'd hurt him without saying so. "Okay, fine. I don't hate persons of a homosexual nature." I looked at him. "And I don't hate you."

He sighed. "Well, I don't hate you, either."

"Thanks."

He paused. "Your father thinks you don't approve of him."

I stuffed my hands in my pockets.

"Do you?"

I looked around, wishing we could just forget the whole episode. "I didn't know this was the Garden of Inquisition."

"It isn't. Just having conversation. You know, light stuff."

"I don't know if I approve of him."

"Why?"

"For a lot of reasons."

"Usually, when somebody says 'for a lot of reasons,' they really mean one or two good reasons they don't want to talk about."

I thought about it. "You know why. We've been through this before."

He nodded. "Sure. But I'm not talking about him getting married, having you, then dropping the bomb fourteen years later even though he knew all along he was gay. I don't approve of that, either. It's unfair to you, your mother, and himself. I'm talking about *being* gay."

I shifted on my feet. "Well then, no, I don't approve."

He nodded. "Tell me why."

"Because I don't want a gay father. That's why."

"Why not?"

I gave him my best "you're out of your frickin' mind" look. "Planet Earth to Edward. You're not *supposed* to have a gay dad. It goes against the whole having-kids thing in the first place, and besides that, it's not cool knowing the only reason you exist is because your dad was lying to himself about shit."

Edward shrugged. "True. So what you're saying is that because he's your dad, that's why you don't approve?"

"I guess. Does that make me devil spawn or something?"

He laughed. "Well, you are devil spawn, but not for that reason."

"Then why are we having this conversation?"

"Because I didn't want to wake up one morning with an ice pick speared through my eye."

"I don't have a problem with you or anybody else, Edward. At least no more than I usually do."

He smiled. "Well, we'll try to act more macho in mixed company." He held up a skinny arm and flexed. "Should I work out, you think? Build some guns?"

"I don't think anything will help you, Edward."

He sighed. "Good, because I detest anything that makes me sweat."

We stood for a moment while he watered the squash. I lit a smoke. "I need help."

He looked at the smoke and smirked his displeasure. "I just helped you. My good deed is done for the day, and I'll get a fever if I continue."

"No, I mean with something else."

"Oh God, what did you do now?" He paused, studying me. "That thing about sheep and lonely men in Montana was a joke. You know that, right?"

"I need to fit in."

He raised his eyebrows for a moment, then narrowed his eyes. "This has to do with breasts, doesn't it?"

I smiled. "Nice ones, too."

He shrugged, then sighed. "And who is the intended victim?"

"A girl down the street. Kimberly Johan. We're going out tonight."

He turned the hose off. "And what, pray tell, are you going to do on this date?"

"Bale hay."

"Baling hay on your first date?"

"Yeah."

He glanced at my hands. "Well, I would ask you how you intend to bale hay with blisters all over your hands, but that might be considered gay, so I won't."

I smiled. "Okay, payback. My hands are fine."

He laughed. "I don't know about you, but baling hay has always been on the top of my best-first-date list. Very romantic."

I shrugged. "I'll take what I can get."

"Sounds like the desperation of a young man in love."

"Whatever." I stuck my hands in my pockets. "She has a dad."

He nodded, looking down at his feet dramatically. "I know this might sound odd, but some heterosexual families actually do have fathers. It's sort of old-fashioned, but every once in a while you'll come across one." He tapped his chin. "In fact, I think you have a father, too. He could talk to you about the birds and the bees and other such things."

Edward always tried to get me to talk to my dad. Edward was a big fan of "communication." I shook my head. "He wears socks with sandals, Edward, and I know about the birds and the bees. That's why I'm going on a date. I need real help."

"This is true. How may I be of assistance?"

"I need new clothes."

He smiled. "Am I hearing Benjamin Campbell say that he actually wants to blend into something?" He leaned close, peering into my eyes. "Are you turning into a conformist?"

I sighed. "What about her dad? Miss Mae said he wouldn't like me, and I'm sure there's all kinds of secret rules and regulations about dating farm girls."

"Ahhh. You must be talking about the proper way to do things when dealing with old-fashioned farm folk, which, I might add, is exactly what Mr. and Mrs. Johan are. If I remember correctly, he's a very harsh man, and one not to cross." He thought for a moment. "Yes sir, no sir, thank you, please, nice to meet you, Mr. Johan, firm handshake, look him in the eye, and for God's sake don't eye her boobs, even accidentally, unless you're at least a mile from the house. Men have shotguns for a reason around here."

I nodded, soaking it all in. Fear gripped me, but love would climb any mountain. "One more thing."

"What?"

"What is baling hay, anyway?"

He laughed. "And you thought you worked hard yesterday. Poor child."

"Crap."

"Shall we go shopping now?"

"Cowboy me up."

He laughed. "You know I'm the last person you should ask to dress you, Benjamin. My taste in clothing fits in around here like the San Francisco Symphony."

We drove into town, stopping in front of the Saddleman, the local clothes place. I looked at Edward in his linen shorts and polo shirt. "There's got to be some redneck left under that sophisticated *GQ* metrosexual veneer. Besides, you know everything about being a fashionista, right? We can do country with class."

He eyed me. "Are you secretly trying to pay me a compliment?"

I laughed. "No, but I want to look right when I'm drinking tea in their parlor."

He rolled his eyes. "One has to know how to drink from a cup to do that, Benjamin."

"Whatever."

He unbuckled his seat belt. "Come on. We've got some outfitting to do."

A man stood behind the counter of the Saddleman, resplendent in Wranglers tight enough to petrify testicles, a colorful cowboy shirt, a handlebar mustache, a cowboy hat, and cowboy boots. You could eat from his belt buckle, it was so big. He looked like every rodeo rider in the history of mankind. Edward knew him. "Hello, Jack. Long time."

The man eyed us, then nodded. "Didn't think you'd be back."

"Some things change."

76

"That they do." He cleared his throat. "Doing some shopping?"

Edward nodded. "For Benjamin. Ben, this is Jack Galladay. We went to school together."

Jack nodded to me, and I remembered, for once, to be polite. I held my hand out. "Nice to meet you, Mr. Galladay."

Jack hesitated, then shook my hand. Hard. The dried blisters on my hand screamed. "You, too, Ben." Then he smiled. "You need any help finding what you want, I'll be around."

Edward looked at him. "Still doing the rodeo?"

Jack shook his head. "Broke my hip five years ago at finals. Three titanium pins holding me together." He gestured to the store. "Bought this place and here I am. Denise runs the back end."

"Denise Reese?"

He looked at Edward for a moment before answering. "Denise Galladay now. We married two years out of school. Four kids."

"Say hello for me," Edward said, and we started looking at the racks of clothes. Jack wandered to the back room.

I lowered my voice. "Was he cool to you in school?"

Edward smiled. "Let's just say some things aren't as they seem."

I glanced at where Jack had gone, then back to Edward. "You mean . . . ?"

He nodded. "Some people question their sexuality a bit more than others."

I couldn't believe it. My dad is a straight gay. He

77

didn't look gay, and you'd never know it until you got to know him. Jack Galladay looked the farthest from a gay dude that I'd ever seen. "No way."

Edward sighed. "I'm not saying what he is now, Ben, and what we did really has nothing to do with anything now. He was a good friend, and I'm sure he's a good husband and father."

Behind all of Edward's sarcastic humor and quick wit, I realized he was good. He didn't hold it over Mr. Galladay's head one single bit. "That's why he looked nervous when we walked in."

"Probably. We were stupid kids, finding out what we were. That's all." Then he smiled, his eyes meeting mine. "I mean, after all, we both became family men."

"Spare me, Mom."

Edward looked at a rack of shirts. "Okay, here's the rules. No gaudy colors, no big belt buckles, and no cowboy hats."

I frowned. "I wanted a hubcap for a belt buckle, man."

He shook his head. "You can't wear a belt buckle like Jack unless you won it in the rodeo. Unspoken cowboy rule."

"Fine. Why no hat?"

"Because you'll look like a complete goof in one."

I shrugged. "Listen, Ed, if I'm going to do this, I'm going all the way. Do they have spurs here? I want spurs. And I want a rope, too. Like a lasso thing."

"Okay, we're leaving. I'm getting stomach cramps just thinking about you walking down the street dressed like Howdy Doody."

I smiled. "Hey, if I'm going to lasso me a mare, I've got to be able to stay in the saddle."

He gave me a disgusted look. "You watch yourself around her father. And it might do you a small bit of good to lift yourself out of the gutter sometimes."

"I was kidding. Lighten up."

He looked at me, a serious question in his eyes. "Did you have sex with Hailee?"

The difference between my dad and Edward was right here, right now. He wasn't afraid to talk about anything. "Of course we did. No woman can resist my touch."

He held up a shirt, grimaced, then put it back. "And now, ladies and gentlemen, Ben will return to reality."

I rolled my eyes. "Okay, fine. No, but almost. Like a rounding-third-and-heading-home kind of deal. We *were* going to be married, you know."

He nodded. "Just do me a favor and make sure you're ready. It's an important thing, not just a feel-good thing."

"This coming from a guy who fooled around with his buddy in the woodshed."

He sighed. "Everybody makes mistakes, and everybody has regrets. Just keep it in mind that women aren't the only ones who can lose their self-respect."

"Will do."

"You should talk about things like this with your father."

I shook my head. "Tell that to him. Every time I do, he wants to turn it into some kind of lesson on life." I looked at him. "Sort of like you're doing now."

"I'm not your father, and because I'm not, I can say whatever I want. And don't go around thinking that I actually care about you or anything, because you're nothing more than a nuisance to me."

"Blah blah blah." I looked around. "Am I going country, or are you going to keep preaching?"

An hour later, I walked out of the Saddleman wearing tan ropers, which are lace-up cowboy-type work boots (you can't work in regular cowboy boots, apparently), a pair of straight-leg Wranglers that made me feel like my nuts were wrapped in duct tape, and a neutral-colored button-up work shirt that gathered the heat like a blowtorch in my waistband. Three pairs of regular Levi's, leather work gloves, and three shirts bulged in the Saddleman bag I carried.

At my insistence, I had also picked out a cowboy hat. Edward smirked disgustedly every time he looked at it. I felt like I should be trick-or-treating, but I also thought it was sort of cool. Like a uniform or something. Maybe Edward was right. Maybe I was conforming. He told me I was conforming to lust.

When we got home, Dad was sitting on the front porch with a file in his lap. We'd made one other stop along the way, and Edward had loaned me some money. I'd purchased something for Billy, but left it in the van for now. I'd give it to him later. Dad looked at me when I got out of the car and gaped. "What happened to my son? Edward? Is he sick?"

Edward smiled. "Love is in the air."

Dad leaned back. "Oh. Enough said. You look nice, son."

Miss Mae banged out the door, a scowl on her face and her hands on her hips, ready to breathe fire about something or other. Flinty eyes riveted on me, and she closed her mouth. Then she walked down the stairs and looked me up and down like I was a cow at auction. She nodded, brought her hands to my collar, straightened it, pressed the lapels down, and patted them with gnarled hands. "Very handsome." Then she turned around and walked up the stairs, muttering about me possibly turning out human.

As she reached the screen door, she turned around. "You get your chores done or I'll make you wish you had a suit of armor on instead of those new duds, boy. I ain't foolin' around, either. I'll switch those stitches into your skin if you make me say it again."

CHAPTER 9

*I*n regular–person speak, what Miss Mae meant was that I had to get my chores done before I went on my work date or I'd be bludgeoned with a giant-size wooden spoon. I went inside, stuffed the rest of my new clothes in my dresser, and walked out back.

When Miss Mae wrote on my chore list that I needed to paint the fence, I didn't realize I had to *fix* it before I did. Twenty feet of it lay on the ground. I found a hammer and a can of nails in the woodshed, grabbed the shovel, looked around for the wheelbarrow, and remembered that Billy had borrowed it.

As I walked across the lawn, I heard the familiar banging of bricks being dropped into the metal tub of the wheelbarrow. I shook my head on my way over, thinking about Billy getting strapped because I'd helped him.

I knew it before I saw it, and as I came around the corner, I saw Billy loading bricks. Mr. Hinks's car was gone. My stomach crawled. "Hey, Billy."

He looked up, didn't say anything, then bent to his work.

I took a breath. "Is he gone?"

He nodded, not looking at me.

"He's making you move them back to the first pile, isn't he?"

He stood up. "You dumb or something? Stay away from me."

"It's not your fault, Billy. You know that, right?"

He kept piling bricks in. "Don't look like it matters much, do it? You ain't from here an' you don't know nothing."

My guts crawled even more. I watched a stray cat slink along the fence line, remembering it as the one who'd rubbed itself between my calves the first day we'd arrived. Charcoal gray. I'd seen Billy petting it the other day on his back porch, playing cat's-paw with it. "I know I'm not from here, but it wasn't your fault and I'm sorry."

Billy straightened, a broken brick in his hand, his sweaty face contorted. I couldn't tell if there were tears in his eyes or if it was just sweat. " 'Sorry' don't cut it around here, faggot. My dad's right. You prob'ly just want to put it in me, like he says."

I'd dealt with stuff before, but never in my face like this. "Whoa. Not even, man. And your dad is an asshole for even saying it."

Billy's eyes swept to the cat slinking along the fence. He walked a few steps to the back door, opened it, then reached inside. He brought out a rifle.

My stomach fell to my feet, images of being blown away by an eleven-year-old boy flashing through my head. "Hey, man, put that away."

He looked at me like I was the biggest dork in the

world, levered a round into the rifle, took aim, and shot the cat. It jumped, then crumpled to the ground. The shot echoed, but it wasn't that loud. Not like I expected it to be.

I stared. "Dude, no way. Why'd you just do that?"

He stared at the cat. "Ain't your business." With that, he walked over to the cat and nudged it with the barrel.

I'd seen my fair share of bad shit back in Spokane, but I'd never seen somebody kill something for no reason, like this kid had just done. I looked at him. There was no feeling in his eyes. Complete indifference that he'd killed a living thing. I pointed to the cat. "There was no reason to do that, man. None."

He put the rifle back inside the door. "Ain't your business."

I stared at the cat. Blood seeped from its mouth. This kid was whacked in the head, and I couldn't believe I'd just seen him do what he'd done. "That was wrong. Totally wrong."

He shrugged. "Stray."

"You were playing with it the other day; I saw you."

He ignored me. I stood there staring at him for a moment, but his face was as blank as a sheet of paper. I turned around and walked inside.

Dad was sitting at the table, with paperwork spread out in front of him. I slouched into a chair. "That kid over there is a nutcase."

He looked up. "How so?"

"He just shot a cat. Didn't you hear it?"

"I thought it was a firecracker."

Miss Mae walked through the room, not bothering to stop. "Subsonic .22. Good for pests." Then she disappeared. Apparently everybody who lived more than five miles out of a city was a firearm expert.

I stared at Dad. "I'm clicking my heels three times, Dad." I closed my eyes, then opened them. Still here. "This place is not right."

Dad stood up. "Is he still out there?"

"Yeah. His dad is making him move all those bricks back for no reason." I gave him a look. "You know, building a work ethic."

"I'll be right back."

A few minutes later, Dad came back in and sat again, staring at the table.

"What happened?"

"Not much."

"What did he say?"

"Well, after he told me to go away, he told me that there were strays all over the place."

"So he should shoot them? God, Dad, we're not talking pellet gun here, and I don't care if it's a sub-whatever .22, it's a rifle. Like a real one."

He shook his head. "I'm not concerned about the cat, Ben, I'm concerned about him."

"I told you Mr. Hinks is screwed up. He beat the crap out of him with a belt right at the back door yesterday because I helped with the bricks."

"You'd better get your chores done."

I stared at him. "What?"

"I'll take care of it."

"Of what? Billy?"

"Yes. I said I would take care of it, and I will."

I knew my dad too well. Ever since I was a little kid, he had to follow the proper rules and regulations, and he never took anything else into consideration. Like Billy getting it double if the authorities were called. "If you call the sheriff, he'll beat the crap out of him again, Dad. You can't."

Dad's eyes sharpened. "I said I'll take care of it."

I walked outside. I could hear Billy moving the bricks, and I stood by the garage for a few minutes, listening. The kid had busted that cat like it was nothing. He'd killed it because it was there, and it slid off his back easy as anything.

I imagined him over there, spending another four hours working because of me, and I couldn't figure out if I felt sorry for him or not. I sat on the back-porch steps and lit a smoke, glancing over at the house every few seconds. Why should I feel sorry for him? I didn't really think you could call it murder, but that was the closest thing to it that I could think of, and besides, it wasn't any of my business anyway. Miss Mae was right. I *should* stay away. But I wouldn't.

I snuffed my butt out and walked over to the minivan, grabbed a bag from the backseat, and went next door. Billy looked at me, dumped the wheelbarrow on the pile, and turned around, trundling over to the old pile. I set the bag down on the bricks, calling to his back, "You can put it in our woodshed if you don't want him to know I gave it to you." Then I walked back home.

I decided to mow the lawn because first of all, the motor would drown out the sound of the damn bricks, and second of all, I needed the wheelbarrow to dig post-holes for the stupid fence, and I wasn't about to go over and get it. Twenty minutes into trying to get the mower started, I knew why people wore boots to work in. They were good for kicking things that didn't work right.

I finally got the thing started and mowed like a mad-man, my arms aching from the day before and my hands killing me. I had two hours before the hay date, and I wanted to take a shower before I walked down to Kimberly's house.

The mower didn't have a bag on it, so I had to rake, and by the time I got done with the backyard and moved back to the front to rake, I saw the sheriff pulling up in his truck. My dad had called. Leave it to him to do things properly.

The sheriff got out, nodded to me, and walked down the Hinkses' driveway. "Hey, Billy, your daddy around?" he called.

I listened from the yard, and Billy answered. "No, sir."

"Come on down here for a minute, huh?"

Billy came down. The sheriff glanced at me, and I started raking. He turned to Billy. "How ya doing, partner?"

"Fine, sir."

The sheriff leaned down, his hands on his knees, and looked into Billy's eyes. "Daddy coming home soon?"

"He said six."

The sheriff looked at his watch, then at Billy. "Your daddy whip you yesterday, son?"

Billy nodded.

"On your bottom?"

He shook his head. "No, sir."

"You just turn on around and let me take a peek, then."

Billy shook his head.

The sheriff took off his sunglasses. "Turn around, Billy." The sheriff twirled his finger as he said this, and Billy did, turning around and looking over his shoulder. The sheriff hooked a finger under the shirt and lifted it. I could see the welts from where I was. It almost hurt just looking at them. He studied the marks. "You get in trouble?"

"Yes, sir."

The sheriff lowered the shirt and turned him around. "For what?"

"Bein' bad."

"Like what kind of bad?"

Billy glanced at me. "Not doing my work the way I was supposed to."

"You shoot a cat today?"

Billy nodded.

"Particular reason?"

"Strays get into the garbage and the garden. Make a mess."

The sheriff nodded. "Fair enough." Then he sighed, taking a minute. "I'll tell you what. You abide what your father says from now on, okay?"

"Yes, sir."

He straightened up. "Get on back to work, then."

Billy walked back, and the sheriff turned toward his truck.

I stopped raking and called to him: "You know what's going to happen if you talk to Mr. Hinks!"

He looked at me, then stopped walking. A moment passed. "What's that supposed to mean?"

"You know what it means, Sheriff. He'll just get more of the same."

He took a toothpick from his breast pocket and popped it in his mouth, hitching his belt up. "I suppose I don't know that." Then he tipped his hat to me. "Take care."

As I watched him go, I realized one thing: Billy Hinks was alone in this world, and nobody cared about it. I couldn't keep my mouth shut. "Sheriff?" He turned. "So you can just shoot shit around here any time you feel like it?"

He smiled. "This isn't the city, Ben."

CHAPTER 10

*B*y the time I got out of the shower, got dressed, and went downstairs, it was four-thirty. I didn't want to be late, and I realized I wouldn't be having dinner, so I grabbed a couple pieces of bread from the bread thing, spread some peanut butter on them, and walked out, saying goodbye to whoever was around to hear it. Miss Mae called to me from her room: "Get in here." I walked to her door, looking in. She sat in a chair by the window, reading a book. She looked up. "You have manners at that Johan house, understand? I won't have my good name smeared around this town on account of some boy who don't know no better."

"Your name is different than my name. Me Campbell, you *Evil*."

She snapped her book shut, fire in her eyes. "I don't need *you* to tell *me* what my last name is, and the first day I do, I'll be in a pine box being laid to rest next to my dead husband. Now get. And don't smart off to me."

"Yes, ma'am."

As I hit the lawn, I saw Billy out by the curb, on the

skateboard I'd left him. The bag lay crumpled on the driveway. He glanced at me, then hit the board, skating a few feet before hitting a pebble and tumbling to the pavement. Just then an old Ford Bronco, with three guys in it around my age, passed, slowing as it came by Billy. One of the passengers, a guy with blindingly white, straight teeth and a high school baseball cap, leaned out the window and smiled. The Bronco idled next to Billy. "Hey, freak, you all right?" The other guys laughed.

Billy stood up, shifting from one foot to another and looking anywhere but at them. The guy laughed again. "Your daddy know you're in the street, scaring people? Get inside, boy!" More laughter ratcheted from the Bronco.

Right then Miss Mae's voice cackled from behind me: "Ronald Jamison, you get off my street an' leave that boy alone 'fore I call your daddy and have you strapped for bein' the no-account you are! You hear me?"

Ronald Jamison laughed; then the driver goosed the Bronco and they were gone. I turned, giving a questioning glance to Miss Mae. She shook her head disgustedly and tottered inside, slamming the screen door shut.

As I passed Billy, he ignored me. "They hassle you a lot?" I asked.

He didn't look up. "I ain't supposed to talk to you."

"Then don't." I walked on.

"Hey."

I turned.

He picked up the board, looking away. "It's cool."

"Yeah." I started walking again.

"Hey."

I turned.

He looked at my outfit, then at my cowboy hat. "That hat ain't gonna do."

I smiled, then tipped my Stetson to him and moved on down the street.

Kimberly's house, like so many other places in the town, was a three-story Craftsman with a porch running along the front. Kimberly's truck was parked outside. I walked up the steps, took a deep breath, and knocked. A minute later, a hulking blond giant with arms bigger than my legs answered the door. From the worn shit-kickers on his feet to the John Deere cap on his head, he was corn-fed trouble if I ever saw it. Except he wasn't Kimberly's dad. Way too young.

He had the same eyes as Kimberly and the same blond hair, but from there the resemblance ended. I didn't know if they had the same smile, because he wasn't smiling. He was looking at me like I was a stray cat in Billy's rifle sight. I took a deep breath. "Hi. Is Kimberly here?"

"Who wants to know?" His voice had all the menace and depth of a killer, just without the German accent.

His body took up the whole doorway. My first thought was to tell him I had come from the church to pick her up to go pray for refugee children. "Ben. Campbell. I . . ."

Then a voice from heaven called from somewhere in the house: "*Dirk!* Leave him alone! *Dad!*"

Footsteps through the living room brought another

male to the door. This one wasn't six-four and menacing. This one was around fifty years old, balding, pudgy, and wearing office slacks and a white-collared button-up shirt. He looked like an accountant, with his round face and round glasses. He had the same eyes as the guy who looked like he was going to stomp me into the porch. I realized Edward had been playing a game with me. Big Boy moved out of the way.

The older man held his hand out. "You must be Ben. I'm Mr. Johan."

I shook his hand, refusing to wince, because any sign of weakness in front of Dirk would mean he'd eat me. Though Mr. Johan's shake was rock hard, there wasn't a callus on his hand. "Nice to meet you, sir."

Dirk looked at my hat and smirked, shaking his head and mumbling something about a clown as he disappeared into the house. Mr. Johan scooted me in. I couldn't help but think he looked like a well-dressed and genteel Mr. Potato Head, then banished the thought because Dirk might be some sort of psychic redneck and smash me with a sledgehammer.

The first thing I noticed was the cows. At least a hundred porcelain miniatures were spread throughout the living room. Pink, blue, black-and-white, polka-dotted— they sat on shelves and tables and glass-encased boxes. Somebody in this house had a clinical fetish for bovines, and it scared me. Mr. Johan took a seat in a recliner, looking at my hat. "Have a seat, Ben."

I did, picking the chair closest to the door in case I had to run. I tried not to stare at the weirdness of the cows. "Thank you." I figured the safest bet was to keep it simple. One-word answers. That way I couldn't say anything stupid.

Mr. Johan noticed my eyes wandering, but he kept staring at my hat. "Mrs. Johan likes cows."

I nodded. "Nice."

He smiled, a joke in his eyes. "If you like cows."

He waited for me to say something, but for the life of me, I couldn't think of anything intelligent to talk about. "I like cows."

He sat back, crossing one knee over the other and folding his hands like my old shrink, Dr. Fruitloops, did back in Spokane. "You look nervous."

"I always do. It's a thing with me."

He gave a short laugh. "Kimberly's brother can come on strong."

Edward's manners class pounded through my head, but I was totally flustered. I have a tendency to say what's on my mind when I'm out of sorts. My palms were sweating. "I'm sure he wouldn't kill me. Maybe just maim me."

This time Mr. Johan laughed outright. "Dirk is nineteen. He works for Mrs. Johan's sister in Wyoming, busting horses. He's visiting."

"Oh." Hopefully he'd be leaving in six or seven minutes.

"Kimberly tells me you're interested in courting her."

I shook my head. "I just want to date her, sir."

He looked at me. "Excuse me?"

"I'm not that kind of guy. Really. We're going to bale hay."

He smiled. " 'Courting' means 'to take out,' Ben. 'To date.' "

"Oh." I looked anywhere but at him, and it looked like it was back to being the social retard of the year.

"You're from Spokane, right?"

I nodded.

"How do you like it here?"

"Well, I hated it until yesterday."

He laughed. "It must be difficult to come to such a different place."

I shrugged. "It's not really that bad. Hot."

He looked me up and down. "You seem to have changed your appearance since arriving."

"Well, Kimberly said we'd be doing work, so my stepdad took me shopping today at the Saddleman."

He raised his eyebrows. "Your stepdad?"

"Edward. My dad's husband. You know him, right?"

Mr. Johan took a breath, then smiled. "Yes. Eddie. He's a bit younger than me. Very interesting circumstance for you, I'd bet."

"I'm fine as long as I take my medication. No violent outbursts, anyway."

He stared blankly at me.

"I was joking, sir."

He broke into a grin. "Oh, I see. Yes. A joke."

Just then Kimberly came downstairs and saved me. I stood up. "Hi."

She smiled, then stared at my hat. "Hi. Ready? We're late."

Mr. Johan walked us to the door, shaking my hand

again and telling Kimberly she should be home by nine. We walked to her truck, and when I got in, my hat hit the roof and fell into the gutter. She looked at me and smiled when I picked it up. I closed the door. "So, why is everybody staring at my hat?"

She took a baseball cap from the seat next to her and put it on. "My dad?"

"And your brother. They were looking at it like it was a lava lamp or something."

"You wore it inside."

"So?"

She smiled. "You're not supposed to wear hats inside. My parents are sort of proper."

"Oh. Sorry." I glanced at it sitting on my lap. "Is it dorky?"

She burst out laughing. "It's the goofiest thing I've ever seen."

"I thought you'd like it."

She put the truck in gear and drove. "I like the spikes better."

"Really?"

"Yeah. They're different."

The image of our kids switched to them running around with spiked hair. "Everybody here has to do the same things and look the same way, don't they?"

She paused, then said, "This is a pretty conservative place."

I rolled my eyes in agreement. "The three of us go over well here, huh?"

She giggled. "Like a fart in church."

"What?"

She laughed. "Never mind. It's just a saying. My uncle says it all the time."

"You didn't tell me you had a brother."

She smiled, shifting into third. "I have a brother. There. I told you."

"He's . . . big."

She nodded. "He's just a typical big brother. Protective of me."

"I don't want to have sex with you."

She laughed. "What?"

"I mean, you can tell him that. You know, just baling some hay. Nice innocent stuff. Tell him I'm a eunuch or something."

She sighed. "I can take care of myself, thank you very much."

"So, you *do* want to have sex? Because if you do, it'd be fine, but I usually don't do that on the first date."

She laughed. "You just say whatever comes into your head, huh?"

"Ben's lifelong problem."

She glanced over at me. "You look different. I'm surprised."

"Why?"

"Because you don't seem to be the kind of person to conform so easily."

I didn't tell her that the only reason I would conform to anything was the female gender. "Well, I thought, When in Rome, do as the Montanans. And we are going to work. I needed boots and stuff."

"You're funny."

"Thanks. It makes up for being ugly."

She giggled as we hit the edge of town, and then looked over at the horizon. Clouds had gathered like huge, filmy cotton balls. "It's going to storm."

"It actually rains here? I thought it was like the Gobi Desert or something. Rain every hundred years."

She smiled. "Oh, it does. Comes in quick, too." She looked again. "You haven't seen a summer storm here, have you?"

"Nope."

She sped up. "We'd better hurry."

As we drove, the silence made me edgy. "You know Billy Hinks, right?"

"Sure. Why?"

"What's their deal, anyway?"

"Let me guess. Mr. Hinks doesn't like you."

"Yeah. He's pretty harsh on Billy."

"Sort of a bad situation. Dad says that ever since Mrs. Hinks left, Mr. Hinks has been bitter. Angry a lot of the time."

"She left, right?"

"Yeah. One night. Just up and left. Nobody even saw it coming. She was quiet, though. Never talked much to anybody."

"People around here don't like them too much, do they?"

She looked at me. "They're sort of weird, I guess."

I told her about the three guys in the Bronco.

She grunted. "Greg Thompson, Ron Jamison, and the tagalong, Cobie Wilson."

"Let me guess. The town bullies."

She shook her head. "Not really. Ron can be a jerk

sometimes, but Greg is nice. Cobie just does whatever Ron does."

I tried to remember what Greg, the driver, looked like, but couldn't. "Greg is nice, huh?"

"Yeah. We dated for a little bit before school let out."

"Past tense, right? Like in 'date-*ed*'?"

She smiled. "Whoa. Slow down there, boy. We're going baling, not on a honeymoon."

I smiled. "Well, it is a kind of date. I just like to know the field, you know? Know who I'm up against."

She laughed, but there was an undercurrent of gloom. "I think I'm the one who decides who I date, Ben Campbell, and I'll tell you one thing: I don't date jealous guys."

I backed off. "So, what's the deal with beating kids with belts around here?" I told her about Billy.

She shrugged. "That happens."

"Yeah, but generally speaking, it's considered child abuse."

"People do things differently around here. It's not like the city, where kids can do whatever they want."

I remembered the sheriff. And my dad. I was getting sick of the whole "different" thing. "Oh, so that's the excuse? We-all 'round here do stuff different-like, so you jus' keep yer nose outta our biznass?"

She drove in silence for a minute, then set her chin. "No, as a matter of fact, it's not that way."

I told her the whole story, including killing the cat. "So you think that putting welts on a kid's back for basically what amounts to talking to me is fine?"

She looked straight ahead. "No, I don't. But that's

not the point. Billy did something he wasn't supposed to, and he got in trouble for it."

I didn't buy it. "So you got strapped when you were a kid?"

"No. Daddy doesn't strap girls. Dirk got it, though. A few times."

"I don't know. It just seemed . . . mean."

"Was it that bad?"

"Bad enough that my dad called the sheriff."

"Really?"

I nodded.

"What did he do?"

"Looked at the welts, then told Billy to do what his dad says from now on."

She hesitated. "Well, if the sheriff saw them, I'm sure it's fine."

"What was his mom like? Usually the mom takes the kid when she splits."

She raised an eyebrow. "Like yours?"

"I said 'usually.' What was she like?"

"Nice. She used to walk Billy to the park and stuff all the time. They kept to themselves mostly, though. Her family was Jehovah's Witness, and they sort of disowned her when she went Pentecostal. Daddy says she probably had enough of both and just left. Couldn't take it anymore."

CHAPTER 11

*W*e drove in silence for a long time, then, and when Kimberly turned onto a dirt driveway, I saw the farm. The barn was bigger than the house. "That's a big barn."

She smiled. "Can't turn back now, city boy."

"Just saying." As we came around the corner, I saw a huge flatbed truck stacked with bales of hay. "I thought we were going to bale hay."

"We are."

I pointed. "That's full. They're already made."

She laughed. "Did you think that we'd make them ourselves? Machines do that. It's our job to take them into the barn."

The stack suddenly grew. "Like with a machine?"

"No, like with our hands. Come on."

We walked up to the truck, and there was a note taped to the driver's-side window. Kimberly read it, then nodded. "My uncle's tractor broke down near Grogan's Flat."

"Where's that?"

She pointed past the farmhouse. "Six hundred acres that way."

An acre could be a mile, for all I knew. "So what do we do?"

She looked at the sky. The clouds we'd seen from the highway were now piled like a wall of black over the farmhouse, ominous and huge in the big sky. "We get the tarps out."

I looked at the clouds over the house. "For us?"

She ran into the barn, calling to me, "For the hay! Come on, I want to get this done and get out to Uncle Morgan."

"Why?"

She pointed to the storm. "It's going to be big. They come on fast and can be dangerous."

I followed her into the barn, the musty smell of heat and hay filling my lungs. "Just call him."

She went to a corner and grabbed a heavy-duty green tarp. "No service out there, and he leaves his phone home most times. He's sort of old-fashioned."

Just then a boom of thunder hit my ears. Not a rumble or a crack, but an *explosion*. I jumped as the rafters shook, filaments of hay falling on my head. "You weren't joking, were you?"

She ran outside. "Grab those straps!"

I looked around, feeling like a dork again, and saw a bundle of straps hanging on the wall near the tarps. I wrapped my arms around them and ran out just as the rain hit, and just like everything else in Rough Butte, it didn't just start, it made a statement. One second it was dry; the next I was getting pummeled. The drops were so big and coming down so fast, it almost hurt. I was instantly drenched.

Kimberly heaved the tarp on top of the fifteen-foot wall of hay, then grabbed ahold of the bale wires and clambered to the top. The rain came down so hard, I could barely see the farmhouse fifty yards away, and then she was yelling at me again. "Get the other tarp and throw it up to me!"

I dropped the straps and ran to the barn, fumbling with my gloves before I took the tarp out and tried to throw it to her. She'd made it look like a piece of cake, and as I threw the heavy thing again, I nearly ripped the muscles from my shoulders trying. It made it, though, and she started spreading it across the back half of the hay. The sides flapped down, blowing in the wind as the world lit up like a strobe light.

Half a second later, the thunder shook my teeth. I stood there, looking up at her, almost in awe as this beautiful and willowy girl danced back and forth on a fifteen-foot-tall mountain of hay in the most hellacious storm I'd ever been in.

"Get the straps and attach them to the corners and along the bottom!" she yelled, the pour of the rain muffling her voice as she worked. "There's hooks on the edge of the truck to attach them! Hurry!"

It took me a second to untangle the straps I'd thrown on the now muddy ground, and another second to find the hooks on the truck. They had it set up so you didn't have to tie anything, and there was a buckle you pulled on to cinch the strap tight. I yanked, then ran around the truck to the other side, doing the same. Kimberly climbed down and we piggybacked each other, going down the line and securing everything.

By the time we got done, I knew I should have been freezing cold, but I wasn't. My heart hammered in my chest like a mallet. The rain hit like ice balls, and the temperature had dropped thirty degrees in a matter of minutes. We ran to the pickup and hopped in, Kimberly firing it up and turning on the heater.

I couldn't hear the engine run for the racket drumming down on the hood and the top of the cab, and as I wiped the water from my eyes, she flipped on the wipers full blast and put the truck in gear. I looked out the window. I'd never been in a storm so bad that the water splashing *up* from the ground made a hazy fog up to the bumper of the truck. I shook my head as another boom of thunder vibrated through us. "This is crazy."

Kimberly, cranking the wheel and giving it gas, didn't crack a smile. "It's not over."

"Where are we going?"

"Grogan's Flat. Uncle Morgan is still out there."

"Won't he just come home?"

She shook her head. "You don't know Uncle Morgan."

I supposed that meant the guy would stay out no matter if the world cracked in half and swallowed him whole. The rain poured harder, almost to the point where you couldn't see even with the wipers going full bore, and as Kimberly took a right onto a dirt trail going through the fields, she slowed.

Mud sucked at the tires and she downshifted, then yanked on a shorter stick shift near the floorboard. The truck jerked. "What's that?"

"Four-wheel drive. We might get stuck."

gasp. I was tired of being told to go away. Rivulets of water ran down the slope, filling the trench I was making beside him. "Shit."

He laughed. "Nothing like a good rain."

I began digging under him, scooping out mud as quickly as I could and ignoring his pain as I bumped him with the shovel. Time dragged on forever, and the only way I could tell that it was passing was my shoulders screaming at me, the air that wouldn't get to my lungs, and a dying man cracking jokes about the rain.

So I dug. I dug like a madman until I thought I couldn't do any more; then I dug some more. Morgan leveraged his elbows into the muddy stubble, crying out as he inched himself to the side. "Keep going, boy."

I kept going, and a few minutes later, I leaned over his chest and grabbed his shoulders. "Going to hurt again, but you're going to have to help." Then I yanked, digging my knees in and pulling him out from under the mud. This time he screamed, but in a few seconds we were clear of the machine. He lay panting on his back, his legs a mangled mess of broken bones. I leaned over again and puked, stars coming to my eyes as the rain poured on us.

The lightning and thunder were almost nonstop now, and I eyed Morgan's truck fifteen yards up the hill. "How long will it take for her to get back?"

He closed his eyes, the rain falling on his face as he gasped. More blood seeped from his mouth. "Too long."

I looked at the truck again. "I'll be right back." I staggered to the truck, the mud sucking at my boots with every step and my head spinning. The keys were in

109

it, so I cranked the ignition. I'd driven enough to get around fine on paved streets, but I'd never driven a truck, and I'd certainly never driven one through a mud bog in Eastern Montana. I cursed myself. He'd die if I fucked this up.

The truck was an automatic, thank God, and I put it in gear, taking a minute to turn the lights on and find the wipers. I eased the truck down the slope, letting the idle take it closer to Morgan, then jumped out and ran to him. "Can you help me get you in the truck?"

He looked at the door. "I'll try."

I got behind him and slung my arms under his, helping him to a sitting position. He gritted his teeth and tried to get a foot underneath himself, and I lifted. He screamed again, and we both fell. Then he was silent, his eyes closed. I sat there, gasping and panting and miserable as he lay unconscious next to me. I had to get him in. I couldn't lift him, though. Not with the muck and mud and my arms like wet noodles.

I felt tears coming, and the familiar fear of always messing things up when it meant the most gripped me. No. Not anymore. Ben the screwed-up teenager didn't have a place here. Then I thought of Kimberly's brother smirking at my hat. He'd be able to do this. These stupid rednecks could do anything, and I wasn't about to let this man die.

I moved behind Morgan and hooked my arms under his to try again. My boots slid and sunk into the field as I dragged him toward the truck. My back wrenched painfully, and I felt the muscles popping in my legs. It seemed like it took forever, but I finally got there and opened the passenger door. I reclined the seat as far as it would go and bent over him, feeling his breath on my cheek as I lifted, shoving and pulling and pushing and sliding him up the side of the seat and rolling him into it.

Once he was in the seat, I shut the door, ran around to the driver's side, and jumped in, putting the truck in gear. The four-wheel-drive light glowed on the dash, and I slammed the truck into the lowest gear and eased it down the hill to the track. Then we were going.

I couldn't go too fast, and I felt like an idiot trying to keep the tires on the track, but every side slope brought the truck sliding toward the edge. I did what I'd seen Kimberly do on the way in, steering upslope from my slide and giving the engine gas, and in a few minutes I had things somewhat under control.

Morgan groaned when I accidentally slid into a gully and had to gun the engine, mud flying everywhere as I tore out of it. He opened his eyes. "That hurt like a son-ofabitch."

"Sorry."

He looked down at his busted body. "Funny-lookin' legs, that's for sure. Ain't supposed to be bent that way."

"You'll go over like a fart in church."

He looked at me.

"Kimberly told me you say that all the time."

He smiled weakly. "I suppose I do." He lay silent for a minute. "You never answered me."

I gave it gas and spun up a hill, closer to the farm-house. "What?"

"You like my niece?"

I nodded.

"Gonna have to switch hats. Doesn't suit you."

"I've heard that already. Thanks."

He leaned back and sighed, closing his eyes. "You'll do."

"Don't fall asleep. You hear me?" I reached over and nudged his shoulder.

He nodded. "Just resting."

By the time I reached the farmhouse, the rain had lessened some, and three trucks, one of them the sheriff's, had converged on the place. I recognized Mr. Johan's truck next to Kimberly's, and when he got out, my dad was with him. Another man in Kimberly's truck got out, too, along with Kimberly and her brother, Dirk.

As they ran toward me, it took them a second to realize Morgan was in the truck. The man I didn't recognize ran back to Kimberly's truck and brought back a bag, rummaging through it and taking out a syringe. I glanced at the horizon as the doctor gave Morgan a shot, and I saw clear skies breaking. Kimberly came up to me. "You got him out."

I nodded.

Tears ran down her face. "Thank you."

I shrugged. "No prob. Do it all the time."

She sobbed, then threw her arms around me and kissed my cheek. A kiss was a kiss, sure, but under these circumstances it wasn't the romantic interlude I thought it would be. She whispered that she wouldn't know what to do if he died.

"He'll be okay. The doctor will patch him up, right?"

She looked toward the others. "Yeah. Sure. He'll be fine."

"You country people are different, right? All tough and stuff." I squeezed her shoulder, my eyes flicking to her dad, Edward's words about shotguns flashing through me. "He will be fine, Kim."

I heard the sheriff talking about a helicopter coming in to take Morgan to some hospital, and then my dad was in front of me. His face was lit with panic, and he began to wrap his arms around my rain-soaked and mud-caked body, but stopped, glancing at Kimberly. He backed up a step, nodded, cleared his throat, and looked me up and down. "You okay, son?"

I wiped the mud from my arms. "Yeah. I'm fine."

CHAPTER 12

*M*organ Johan had two broken legs; five broken ribs, two having punctured his lungs; and a broken pelvis. He almost died in surgery that night. I didn't see Kimberly for two days, but her father stopped by to thank me. That evening, I shook his hand, Dad and Edward invited him in for a beer, and they talked for an hour or so about Morgan, life, and Rough Butte.

Two days after that, the town of Rough Butte did something that taught me a lot about this place. They went out to Morgan's farm and cleared his fields for him. A total of seventeen combines, twenty flatbeds, and over one hundred men, their wives and kids, showed up and got three weeks of work done in two days. Morgan's wife, Helen, cooked for every one of them. Miss Mae and several other widows helped her with the food assembly line.

Kimberly invited me on our second date. We spent two days baling hay and doing a bunch of other farm stuff at Morgan's place with the rest of the town. It sucked, but I kissed her on her porch the second day and she liked it. Oh, yeah—I ditched the hat, too, keeping the jeans and boots but settling on my spikes. The bad news was that Dirk was staying at Uncle Morgan's for a while. The dude scared me.

Mr. Hinks didn't participate in helping the Johans. He complained loudly of a sore back, and Miss Mae, ever the opinionated old woman, told him he could help the women.

An odd thing happened to Mr. Hinks about a week after the whole me-saving-Kimberly's-uncle-from-certain-death thing. It seems that somebody, gosh knows who, took all the antlers off his garage wall. I stood at my window, watching him file a report with the sheriff. Billy stood by his father's side with his hands in his pockets, staring at the de-antlered wall.

I closed my closet door, careful not to disturb the fifteen pairs of antlers I'd spent all night cutting off the wall. Norman Hinks could take his pile of bricks and shove them up his ass.

A few minutes later, Miss Mae yelled at me from downstairs. I walked down and the sheriff stood at the front door. Miss Mae stood resolute, her face stony as she stared at me. "Sheriff wants to talk to you." Then she barged out, leaving me with him.

Sheriff Wilkins hooked his thumb in his gun belt. "Miss Mae says your daddy and Edward are out."

"I just woke up."

He eyed me. "Late night?"

I nodded.

"Mr. Hinks is mighty upset about his property being stolen. Says it's twenty years' worth of hunting down the drain."

I shrugged. "Somebody around here must not like him very much."

"Says you did it."

I didn't say anything.

Sheriff Wilkins studied me for a moment. "You're treading a fine line here, Ben."

"With who?"

He tipped his hat up, adjusting it. "Well, with Mr. Hinks for sure. And me. You know if I find out you did it, I have to charge you."

"You don't have to do anything you don't want to do."

He raised his eyebrows, paused, then went on. "You be careful around him, you hear?"

"Maybe you should tell that to Billy."

"I'm not here to discuss Billy. I'm here to warn you. Norman Hinks should be left alone."

After pondering my possible death at the hands of a crazy ex–Pentecostal preacher, I put my gloves on and walked over to the Hinks house, knocking on the screen door. I don't know why I did these things, because the pit of my stomach always contracted and my back tightened, but something inside just compelled me to be an asshole sometimes.

Billy answered, didn't say anything, and ran into the kitchen. A few seconds later, Mr. Hinks came to the door. He stared at me, the vein in his skinny neck throbbing. "You got something to say to me?"

I smiled. "I need Miss Mae's wheelbarrow. Is Billy done with it?"

His eyes were chipped flint, and the skin around that neck vein turned red. "You baiting me, boy?"

"No, sir. Just asking for the wheelbarrow."

His mouth turned into an ugly smear, and I was sure he was about to erupt. But he didn't. He growled that it was in the back, then slammed the door on me.

An hour later, I'd dug the first posthole and had the concrete mixed to set it when Mr. Hinks came out the back door with his keys in his hands. He stared at me over the fence the entire way to his car, got in, and backed out. I smiled and waved as he drove away.

"You are one smart-alecky young man, and I should have your hide for the torment you cause around here."

I turned around, and Miss Mae was standing there. She'd come out every fifteen minutes or so to tell me what to do next, since I'd never fixed a fence before, and now she stood with her hands on her hips, looking at me. I smiled. "I'm good at torment."

She narrowed her eyes, studied my work, then turned back toward the house. "You get those antlers out of my house by tomorrow or I'll strap your backside raw."

I watched her go, my jaw slack in amazement. I should have figured she would snoop in my room, and that didn't weird me out so much. What she'd just said had. She knew, and she wasn't telling.

I went back to mixing the concrete, set a four-foot post in a hole, and poured some concrete into it. Billy came out the back door and grabbed a rake. "Hey, Billy."

He didn't answer, so I bent to my work again, grabbing another post and throwing it to the next hole. As I

117

wheeled the cement over, I looked up and he was standing there, staring at me, his big eyes and big shaved head looking oversized on his skinny body. I ignored him, taking up the shovel and clearing dirt from the hole.

"How'd you do that trick?"

I straightened. "What trick?"

"That one where you spin the board over and land on it."

"A kick spin?"

He nodded.

I glanced to the street. "Where'd your dad go?"

He looked at the driveway. "Car auction in Big Springs."

"Get your board and I'll show you. Meet me." I took my gloves off and watched as he ran over to his house, moved a piece of lattice from the side, and scurried into the crawl space under the porch. I went into Miss Mae's house, grabbed my own board, traded my work boots for the worn-out and faded skate kicks I'd had for a year, and came out to the porch. Billy stood in his driveway, his knees dusty from crawling. I laced up my All Stars and met him. I dropped my board. "Your dad going to be mad if he catches us?"

He nodded.

"You sure you want to do this?"

He looked at the board in his hands. "I want to do a trick."

"Okay." I hopped on my board, gesturing for him to do the same. He set it down and stepped on it, wobbly as he tried to gain his balance. I smiled. "You can't learn a kick flip until you learn other things first. It's too hard."

"I can do it. I saw you."

"Okay. Try."

"Do it again so I can see."

I did, pushing off and kicking up the board, spinning it with my toe, and landing on the deck.

Billy pushed off, tried to kick up his board, and fell back flat on his butt, grunting when he hit the pavement.

I smiled. "Hurts, doesn't it?"

He scrambled up, shaking his head no.

"Here, just try doing the kick. Almost like a wheelie on a bike, and you don't have to be moving. Like this." I showed him, and then he tried. He didn't fall on the third try. "Good job. You can turn when you're doing the wheelie." I did a one-eighty. "See?"

He tried it and the rear wheels slid out. Down he went, this time saying "Ouch!" as his hip hit the driveway.

I laughed. "Get used to it. I've burned about a billion times. Everybody does."

He smiled, embarrassed. "I can do it. Watch." He did, then, and stepped the nose of the board over a foot or so.

"Awesome. Just keep doing that and things will start coming. It gets easier." I showed him a couple of other tricks that involved kicking the board and he practiced doing them himself, each time pausing to stare intently at what I did. I stopped for a while, lighting a cigarette and watching him. Then I nodded to the lattice. "Is that the secret place you were talking about? Where you put the stuffed animal?"

He shook his head.

I knew he was lying. "You ever see your mom?"

He didn't answer, but turned his back to me and tried a one-eighty.

"Never?"

"She's gone."

I inhaled. "Mine is, too."

"You got a mom?"

I hopped on my board and did a three-sixty. "Yeah. Everybody does."

He didn't answer for a minute. "Your daddy's a faggot. That means he likes other guys. How'd you get a mom that way?"

Whoa. I wasn't about to give him the birds-and-bees talk. "He wasn't always that way. He had a wife, and they had me."

"Pa says he'll go to hell for it."

"Maybe so. You think so?"

He shook his head. "I don't know. Bible says so, though."

"I heard the Bible says you go to hell for killing cats."

He picked up his board. "Ain't so."

"You like killing them?"

"No."

"Then why do you?"

"Pa says so. Calls 'em a nuisance." He stood there, holding his board. "Pa thinks you took his antlers."

"Oh."

"Says if he'd a caught you, there'd be hell to pay."

"Too bad he didn't catch the guy."

Billy smiled. "I ain't gonna say nothing."

I stared at him. "About what?"

"That I saw you do it."

Later that afternoon, I changed into my street clothes and grabbed my board. All work and no play made a boring person leading a life of drudgery, and I figured I had enough time in the future to be a miserable drone. I skated down the street, and as I passed Kimberly's house, she came out the door with her keys jangling in her hand. We were at the in-between stage, I guessed, not knowing if we were really dating or just work-dating. She smiled, looking me up and down. "Hey, you're back to normal."

"I'm a complex and multifaceted person. You wouldn't understand."

She opened her truck door. "Well, Mr. Complex Person, would you like to join me for a ride? Mom needs eggs."

"You buy eggs?"

She squinted her eyes. "Well, we don't lay them ourselves."

"Oh. I thought everybody around here bartered and traded. You know, a dozen eggs for some gingham or something."

She grinned. "You are so ignorant sometimes. I swear." Her eyes sparkled. "You coming?"

I threw my board in the bed of the truck and hopped

in, sighing. "Remember our first date? The storm and lightning and sliding farm equipment? God, it was so romantic."

She laughed. "Uncle Morgan is doing fine."

"Good."

She slid me a glance. "So, why haven't you come over?"

I took a moment, watching the neighborhood slide by. "Well, there's this certain person that makes me want to pee my pants every time I see him."

"Dirk?"

"That might be his name."

"Why?"

"Well, because the whole time we were working out at your uncle's place, he never said a word to me. He's got quite a nice glare, though. Very professional. He'll make a great *WWF SmackDown* wrestler someday."

She sighed. "Okay. I'll talk to him. He's really nice once you get to know him." She glanced at me, noticing the skepticism on my face. "Really. He is. I think he'd like you."

" 'Like me' in the sense of adding salt and pepper before dining on my flesh, or 'like me' in the sense of 'Hey, Ben, how's it going?' "

She laughed. "He's not going to hurt you, Ben. I promise. He's a kitten inside."

"Okay. I'll believe you, but don't talk to him, huh? That would be weird."

"Deal."

I tapped my knee. "So does this mean we're dating? Like boyfriend-girlfriend kind of stuff?"

She smiled. "I guess it does."

"Cool."

We reached the store, this one on the far side of town, and Ron Jamison was coming out with a can of chew in his hand as we went in. He looked me up and down, took in the spikes, smiled thinly, then glanced at Kimberly. "Got a new pet, Kim?" Those white teeth flashed, and he winked.

I stuck my hand out, giving him as insincere a smile as I could muster. "You must be Ronald. Ronald, my name is Benald. I saw you bullying that little boy the other day. Pleasure meeting you."

His eyes darkened for just a moment; then he smiled as he shook my hand. "Yeah, sure." He stuffed his lip full of chew, then spit a brown stream at my feet in clear and undisputable aggression. "You coming to the pot-luck, Kim?"

"Yes."

He smiled. "Good deal." His eyes flicked to me. "Greg'll be there, you know."

She looked uncomfortable. "Yeah, I know."

He nodded, hooking his thumbs in his back pockets. "Bring your friend here, huh? Maybe he can show me a few moves on his little skateboard."

After Ronald left, Kimberly didn't say anything. We went in the store. She bent down to pick up some eggs, started giggling, then laughing outright.

I stuffed my hands in my pockets. "What?"

She shook her head. "Benald?"

I smiled. "I guess I got mixed up. Ronald, Benald. I get that way around assholes."

CHAPTER 13

*E*dward hadn't cooked a thing since we'd gotten to Rough Butte, because Miss Mae wouldn't let him. Women cooked. But that night, Dad and Edward got home with news, and Edward insisted on cooking a celebratory dinner before they told us. I sat in the kitchen, watching them, just like I had back home. Miss Mae stomped around the house, dusting and grumbling about her kitchen being overtaken. "If I wanted my son to be a girl, I woulda had a daughter," she snipped as she walked by. My mood matched hers because of the Ronald episode.

I smiled, watching Edward. He was an excellent cook. "So, what's the news?"

Dad was simmering some tomato sauce on the stove. "You'll learn soon enough."

"Let me guess. You guys are having a baby."

Edward laughed. "I'll look fabulous in maternity clothes, Paul. Don't you think? I was thinking of Franklin as the name." He looked at me. "You think, Ben? Then we can introduce you two as Benjamin Franklin."

I rolled my eyes. "How about Brownie?"

Dad frowned. "Enough of the crude stuff, Ben."

Edward turned and mimicked him, shaking his cutting knife at me. I laughed. "Sorry. It just slid out. A no-wiper."

Edward burst out laughing. Dad wasn't impressed. He still got uncomfortable when Edward and I started with the rude jokes, and I liked the disgusting ones. "Knock it off, Ben."

"Sorry. Sometimes I forget to be bland and politically correct about everything. Happy shiny, right?"

He looked at me, and I was surprised he was angry. He held the wooden spoon out, pointing it at me. "Let's not get into that whole thing, okay? What you said was crude and disgusting, and this doesn't have anything to do with political correctness."

I rolled my eyes. "You're such a prude, Dad."

My humor didn't take his anger away. "No, I just expect my son to rise out of that gutter he likes to live in every once in a while and be civil. You push every button you know how to push with me, and I'm getting tired of it." He looked at Edward, who was quiet now. Dad went on. "Is it crazy to expect civility from my son, Edward? Am I a nut? Am I just grasping at straws here?"

Edward smiled. "Paul, it's like buying a cute little puppy that ends up eating its poo. Ben was just born to have a potty mouth."

Dad wasn't in the mood. "Not funny."

Edward laughed, trying desperately to prevent the fight he knew was coming between us. "I know this homophobic issue has been on your mind lately, Paul, but Ben's not homophobic, he's *world*ophobic. He hates everything equally." He glanced at me, a glimmer in his eye. "Right, Ben?"

"Absolutely." I shrugged, looking at Dad. "Are you two done talking about me like I'm not here? I mean, I don't want to get in the way of things or anything, but every once in a while I enjoy my existence being noticed."

Edward smiled. "Get me a beer, then."

I sat back. "You know, I've been thinking. . . ."

Edward slumped his shoulders. "Oh, no, here he goes with that thinking thing again." He looked at me. "How many times have I told you that you're just not meant to do that, Ben? You'll hurt yourself."

"No, really. I think I should be able to have a beer on the porch with you guys."

Dad turned around, and there was an edge to his voice. "I've given you the smoking, but only because of the no-pot issue. No beer until you're twenty-one."

"I'll be eighteen next year, which is probably legal age here, and besides that, I work now. A cold brewski sounds good after being ordered around by Miss Mae all day." I went on before he could say no, thinking that if I could get them to agree, Miss Mae wouldn't have something else to blackmail me about. "Kimberly told me she has a glass of wine at the dinner table with her parents, and she's definitely not out getting blasted every weekend and having sex with boys. At least not with me, anyway."

Edward laughed. "Comparing Kimberly Johan to you is like comparing an angel food cake to a pile of vomit."

I smirked.

Dad contemplated. "Edward? Your thoughts?"

He shrugged. "I think he's earned it. I mean, he is working just about all day, every day now. Besides, Mom wants a new shed built after he's done with the fence." He twirled a utensil. "Not like the labor is going to dry up around here, that's for sure."

I raised my eyebrows at that one, but kept my mouth shut.

Dad faced me. "Fine, then. One beer, but only with me, only here, and only when I say so."

"Deal." I stood and walked to the fridge. "You want one, right, Ed?"

"Sure. The pale ale. And it's Edward."

I scrounged around in the fridge. "Got any Coors? I'm a Coors guy."

Dad warned me: "I can rescind it, Ben. Don't smart off."

I zipped it, grabbed two beers, handed one to Edward, and popped the cap on mine. I took a swig, leaning against the counter. "Ahhh. Nothing like a brew after sweating your butt off all day. I feel like a real man."

Edward laughed. "That's the good thing about feelings. They don't have to be accurate."

I ignored him. "So are you going to tell me what the gig is?"

Dad turned around, nodded to Edward, and spoke. "We're starting a business in town. A restaurant."

"Eddie and Paul's Fried Chicken and Gizzards?"

Edward shook his head. "Foolish boy. A steakhouse. A *gourmet* steakhouse. Your father and I figured that since Montana has the best beef in the entire world and nobody would hire two gay cowpokes anyway, these people should learn how to eat correctly." He waved his spatula. "I'll be the chef."

Edward could cook better than anybody I'd ever known, but that didn't make him a chef. "You're not a chef, though."

He waved the spatula in the air, bowing. "In that way, you are somewhat correct. I did study culinary arts for nearly two years, though. In California. I can hold my own, and besides that, Montanans aren't big on official titles."

"Awesome. If you need a slacker to wash dishes, just ask."

Dad cut in. "We leased the building last week, and we'll start decorating tomorrow. It's sort of small, but sixteen tables should be enough."

"And I suppose you'll need me to help get it ready?"

He shook his head. "You've got your own work."

"What did you name it?"

"Benjamin's"

I raised my eyebrows.

Dad nodded. "We thought it would be a tribute to us coming here."

Edward whisked something in a skillet. "Yeah, since the only reason we moved was to get your butt out of trouble."

I took a gulp of beer. "Benjamin's. I like that. Reminds me of a guy I know. He's amazing."

Dad cleared his throat. "Edward and I were at the bank this morning. Seems the news of the town was about Mr. Hinks getting his antlers stolen." He glanced at me. "Know anything about that, son?"

"Well, when I was out last night stealing all those antlers, I thought I heard something. I could be wrong, though."

Dad turned, an edge to his voice. "Dammit, son. I thought we could start over here. Why?"

I shrugged. "You called the sheriff, I took antlers. Same diff."

"No. Not the same. You broke the law."

I stood. "So did he. Go talk to him if you're concerned about it."

He shook his head. "No dice, Ben. I did what was right, and if the sheriff decides not to do anything about it, I can't help that. I'm not even sure it's legal for a child that age to shoot a rifle."

I rolled my eyes. "Story of your life, Pops. Just blow it off on somebody else so you don't have to worry about it."

Dad stopped stirring. "That's enough with the mouth. I said that's enough, and that *is* enough."

"Yeah, everything is enough. Always enough."

He pointed at me. "Stay away from Mr. Hinks."

Edward wasn't smiling anymore. He'd been around long enough to know when a storm was brewing. "He's right. We did what we were supposed to, and that's enough."

I grunted, sick of it all. "You know what? Both of you are such . . ."

Dad was across the kitchen in a heartbeat, grabbing my shirt and shoving me against the cupboard. Hard. He raised his fist, winding back and ready to hit. "What, Ben? What are we?" His eyes were locked on mine, and

I'd never seen that look in them. This wasn't about antlers at all. This was about my hands and the bank lady and what I'd said before.

His fist landed hard against my chest. Edward gaped, standing stock-still with the spatula in his hand. This had never happened before. Miss Mae walked into the kitchen, probably wondering what the ruckus was, saw Dad pinning me against the cupboard, nodded, then walked back out.

I met his stare. "Go ahead, Dad. Do it. I don't care."

He jammed his fist farther into my chest. "Answer me."

I knew right then that we weren't having a debate about this. This was no learning lesson for Ben Campbell, it was a test. I'd pushed him too far, but he could go to hell. He'd pushed me too far for three years. "Fine. I *will* answer you. You're a pussy."

Dad tensed, then Edward spoke: "Paul, please . . ."

Dad's arm flew toward me and I flinched. His hand slammed into my chest again, and the next thing I knew, my beer was sailing across the kitchen as he jerked me to the back door, pinning me again while he opened it. He yanked me outside and threw me to the ground, his breathing ragged as he raised his fist to me. "Make one more comment and I will, Ben. On my mother's grave, I will not stand for this anymore."

I lay there, looking up at him. "Stand for what? The truth?"

His eyes seared into me as he pointed down the driveway. "Get out."

I stood, screaming as it all spilled out: "To where? You brought me here! You're so full of shit I can't believe

130

it! Oh, we have to go to bumfuck nowhere so Ben doesn't ruin his life? Guess what, Dad, I didn't ruin my life, you did! I'm your lie, man! I'm the big seventeen-year-old reminder that you couldn't stop with screwing up just your own life. No, no, no, you had to have me." I shook my head. "How would you like it, huh? How would you like to know the only reason you exist is because your dad is a selfish rotten bastard who didn't have the balls to face himself! Yeah, sure, I'll go, and you'll never see me again." I turned and had started walking down the driveway along the side of the house when Miss Mae came around the corner from the front porch, blocking my way. Fire lit her narrowed eyes.

I tried walking around her, but she whipped her hand out and cuffed me. Then she grabbed my ear and yanked down, bending me over. Her fingers were like a vise as she dragged me back to my dad, who stood there staring. I was still bent over, looking at the ground, with her pincers on my just-about-ripped-off ear. She growled at Dad, "You need to learn one thing around here, Mr. Paul. You're the man of this house, and I'll be damned to hell if a seventeen-year-old boy will speak to you in this manner in my presence." She yanked me up, her fingers still clamped on my ear. "You two will finish what you started, and you won't come in my home until you come to terms with what got your spines all stiff. Blood don't treat blood with this nastiness."

She walked to the back door, then faced us. Her flowered dress fluttered in the evening breeze. Her eyes glinted. "Maybe you *should* beat the hell out of each other. Teach you both a lesson in manners." Then she was gone, through the door and to whatever sulfur pit she lived in.

Dad and I stared at each other. My ear burned. "I meant every word I said."

Dad didn't back down. His voice was low. "Then you've got to decide if you can live with it."

We stared at each other for several minutes, thinking about what to do. The breeze blew, and dusk fell deeper into itself. Silence, neither of us budging. I shook my head, sitting on a metal drum next to the shed. "It's not that bad out here, really. You can use the garden if you have to take a dump."

He sat on the porch steps. "What's going on here, Ben?"

"You tell me."

"I've explained to you what I did and why I did it. I can't make excuses. We've been through this before."

I shrugged, rubbing my ear. "See, that's it. If it's over for you, it's over for everybody, right? Well, it won't go away for me. I've tried."

"Being gay doesn't mean . . ."

"Dad, it's not all about being gay. You're so caught up in *what* you are that you can't see *who* you are, and it pisses me off. This isn't happening because you love a guy or like men or whatever. You go around on this high horse, saying what's right and wrong for me all the time, but when it comes to you, you do whatever you want."

He shook his head. "No. Let's back up. You think I don't wish my son was different? That he got good grades and played sports and didn't have this huge chip on his shoulder about the whole world? Have you ever wondered if I'm ever embarrassed about you? That's life, Ben, and I do know who I am. Maybe I get wound up and defensive about being gay, but I don't do whatever I want when I want." He gestured around him. "You think I wasn't afraid to come here? That I didn't wonder what would happen to me? To us? You think I've spent my whole life being selfish, and that's fine. But I spent the first fourteen years of your life doing what's best for you, not me, and it's why we're in Rough Butte right now." He studied me. "Ben, you can hate me for it if you want, but it is what it is, and I will not have you or anybody else speak to me the way you did. You may think I deserve it, but Edward doesn't."

"Well, that's the way I feel." I threw a pebble, frustrated. Apparently my dad thought that being a parent stopped after the fourteen-year mark. Then you could do whatever the hell you wanted. I didn't say that, though, because that would be useless. "Maybe we just shouldn't talk about it."

He stood up, and in a flash, a moment in time, my dad showed me where I stood. He nodded. "I am done talking about it, son. This is your problem to come to terms with, not mine." Then he went inside, leaving me to myself.

My dad was never done talking about anything. There was always another hour of getting in touch with feelings and analyzing the situation and giving me advice. Not here, not now, though. I knew how he saw it. This wasn't a dad arguing with his son about stuff. We'd gone beyond that. It was two people parting ways on the way they felt about life. I didn't like it, but I couldn't change it.

After about twenty minutes, I went back inside. Dad and Edward sat at the kitchen table, and their conversation ceased. "Dad?"

He didn't turn around. Edward gave me a pleading look, then got up and walked out. Dad sat there, completely still. "What?" he said.

"I shouldn't have said what I did."

"I told you we're done talking about this, Ben."

"I'm sorry."

"I don't want your apologies."

I stared at the back of his head. "Then what do you want? I'm trying here."

He turned. "Ben, sometimes what you say doesn't go away. It can't be repaired, fixed, or worked out. It's just there."

"What are you saying?"

"I'm saying that I'm not going to live my life feeling this burden of guilt any longer. I can't do it. You'll either accept me or walk away, but I won't listen to my life being condemned by you."

"And you're saying I've crossed that line?"

He slowly shook his head. "No. I'm not. I'm saying that I don't like you very much right now."

I looked at him. At least we had something in common.

Dinner was an absolute misery-fest. Dad was deflated and silent, I didn't have anything to say—I couldn't say I was sorry, because Miss Mae would reach across the table and hit me with something—and Edward got tired of trying to celebrate their business all by himself. The whole night was a dud, and it was completely my fault.

Later I found Edward sitting on the front porch alone, holding a cup of coffee. I sat next to him, both of us watching the moon rise over the houses. "I messed things up," I said.

In the darkness, his voice came soft: "Yes."

"I'm messed up."

Silence.

"It's different this time, isn't it?"

"You're not fourteen anymore."

"I know, but I just get so sick of the way he is sometimes."

"I suppose that's the way families are, you know? We're all different."

"I know, but I just get . . ."

He interrupted me, his voice sharper. "I know exactly what you get, Ben."

"What, then? Tell me, because I don't even know."

He shrugged, taking a sip of coffee. "When I was a teenager, before I moved to Spokane, I remember going places with my dad. You know, like father-and-son things. One time, probably about a month before I left, we went to a Youth Cattleman's party at the Grange. All the men were there with their boys, and I'll never forget it." He paused. "Groups and clusters of fathers and sons talked and visited, and I remember us. Just he and I, standing by ourselves by the refreshment table. We didn't talk, standing there with plastic punch cups in our hands and this mutual feeling that one of us didn't

135

belong there. Both of us knew how I was by then, and so did most of the town. I think it was one last effort on his part and one dying gasp on my part to have a good relationship with each other. The kind you're supposed to have as father and son."

"That sucks."

Edward shook his head, laughing softly. "Not really. My father always loved me. I knew that. I also understood that he just plain disagreed with it, and that wasn't even bad. We could disagree. You know what was bad, though? At that party?"

"What?"

"The look all over his face that said he was ashamed. I'd never noticed it before, but that night I did, and I realized just how embarrassed he was to have a son like me." He looked my way. "You know how it feels when a person you love feels that way about you, Ben? It's just about the worst feeling you can have. Like you just want to shrivel up and die."

I stared into the moonlit sky. "How can I not feel that way, then? Sometimes, when I look at him, I just wish he didn't exist, you know? I do love him, but I can't help it. It's just there."

"When my mother sent me away, I wasn't thrown out. You probably see it that way, but it wasn't. She knew what was best for me, and you know what? It *was* the best for me. I wouldn't be who I am if she hadn't, and I still thank her for it. This place wasn't good for me."

"What about your dad, though? Did he ever see things differently?"

"I think he was glad to see me gone. For my sake and for his sake. He never felt differently, though. He couldn't. And it wasn't that *I* was gay. It was that *he* had a gay son. And when he died, he told me so. It was the first time I'd ever heard my father apologize for anything."

I thought about what Edward had said, and it made me feel even worse, because I knew what he was saying. But I wasn't Dad's father. I was his son. And even though my dad might have not chosen to be gay, he had chosen to be a gay father.

CHAPTER 14

*T*he next morning, Dad and I were walking around ready to pounce on each other like cornered cats, and I was up for breakfast, dressed, and out the door after a few bites of French toast. I had no idea how to make things better, and the way Dad avoided me, even after Edward and I had talked the night before, I couldn't help but feel he was sulking around like a kid who didn't get dessert.

Dad had told me we were done talking about it, and even though a part of me wanted to fold over and grovel, another part wanted to tell him to deal with this like he'd made me deal with everything.

As I sat on the front porch having a smoke after breakfast, I thought about how he'd made me live with it. I hated rules and regulations and authority and all the things that Dad relied on to make his life orderly and safe, and I resented him for trying to force me to be like him. I wasn't.

When Dad came out of the closet and Mom walked out and I flipped out, he made a plan. He would rely on all the safety nets that I considered stupid. He contacted my school counselor, he put me in major professional counseling with Dr. Fruitloops, he put us in family counseling, he bought books—he did everything he could think of to have other people solve our problems—and I hated him for it.

Back then, I hated him for it because he'd ruined our family, but after a while I hated him because *he* didn't want to suffer the consequences of his decision. He wanted *me* to.

The first time he'd caught me smoking pot, he didn't even catch me. There's no catching involved when you do it on purpose, and even at fifteen years old, I knew exactly what would happen—and it did, which made me hate him even more.

He came home from work one day, walked in the door, put his keys on the table by the door, hung his coat in the closet, set the mail in the mail thing, and did what he did every single day when he got home. He called my name. I didn't answer for two reasons. The first was that I wanted him to come to my room, and the second was that I was so baked I could barely talk in sentences.

He should have smelled it two blocks away, but he didn't, and when he opened my door, the thick haze of smoke shrouded him in the doorway. He asked what I was doing. I offered him a hit.

Now, if that had been my mom at the door, or even my dad before he decided to come out of the closet, there would have been hell to pay. I would have been strung from the rafters for a week. I would have been grounded. I would have had to do a zillion hours of chores. I would have been monitored by the minute for the next year.

Dad turned around and walked out. I went to school the next day, and my student counselor spent an hour talking to me about using drugs. Dad had called him. That night, after Dad got home, a police officer showed up at our door. Dad had arranged a "meeting" with our school's resource police officer, and Mr. Cop spent another hour talking to me about what would happen if I got caught. I wouldn't want a record, would I? I wouldn't want to start that spiral into the darkness of criminality, would I? He didn't know me very well.

After the cop left, Dad sat me down and calmly explained to me why I was doing what I was doing, and that while he understood there would be bumps in the road such as this, if he found drugs in the house again he'd call the police and have me arrested. Apparently, breaking the law was much worse than tearing a family apart.

That was the difference, I thought bleakly. Before it all happened, the only thing my dad had to worry about was me chewing gum in class, and the only thing I looked forward to was coming home to a dad who would pat me on the shoulder, smile, and tell me there were worse things than chewing gum. Then we'd go out and play catch, and Mom would take the gum from my backpack while we did.

Now we were in Rough Butte, and I knew well enough that this town was just another way for my dad to have a problem solved by something besides himself. The last exit to normal for a family that would never be normal. He'd given up on everybody in Spokane that couldn't make us the way we used to be, so he'd taken the whole city out of the picture. Great.

But I knew it wasn't all that way. I knew he loved me, and I didn't give a crap about what normal was or wasn't, but things were different in a more serious way. A more personal way. He'd told me he didn't like me, and for some reason, that hurt more than any screaming match we'd ever been in or any anger he'd ever shown. I'd spent so long not liking him, I wasn't used to him not liking me.

I thought about the look in his eyes when he'd slammed me against the cupboard, and I shook my head. It was the closest thing to hate I'd ever seen coming out of him, and it was directed at me. It was almost like the true Paul Campbell showed himself to me.

After deciding I was thinked out about the whole stupid thing, I'd dug the last of the postholes for the fence and had begun nailing the boards to the frame when Billy came out. Mr. Hinks's car was gone, and as Billy grabbed a shovel and came near the fence, I stopped working. "Hey, Billy."

"Hey." He picked up the stiff and dead cat with the shovel.

I watched him.

He turned, balancing the cat on the blade. "They get stiff after a coupla days." He started walking toward the fields behind the house. I watched. Both Miss Mae's and the Hinkses' backyards ended with a wire fence bordering open fields. Billy opened the rickety wire gate leading

141

into the field, humming a slow song as he walked carefully over the rough terrain, the cat's glassy eyes staring at the horizon like it wished for something other than a bumpy ride on a shovel.

I dropped my hammer and followed, staying back. A stand of stunted pine trees, dry and dusty and off in the distance, jutted into the sky just before a hollow led down to a dry creek bed. As he entered the trees and walked down the ravine, I paused, watching him. He stopped then, as if getting his bearings, and headed to the left and farther down. Twenty yards on, he stopped again, set the cat down, and studied the rocky ground for a moment.

I crept to the edge of the trees, watching as he found the spot he was looking for and began digging. Flash floods from years ago must have unearthed and tumbled the rocks here, and they lay scattered and piled on the baked soil. Billy wiped his forehead, digging for ten minutes or so before setting the shovel down.

I knew what he was doing, but didn't know why. He'd killed the cat as easily as wiping a booger on his sleeve, and now, seeing him gently lift the cat and put it into the grave, I wondered what this kid's deal was. A few minutes later, he'd filled the hole and began piling rocks on it carefully, almost reverently. He finished, and the burial mound was complete.

I looked along the length of the ravine, and that's when I noticed. A chill ran up my spine. Floods hadn't piled those rocks, and they weren't helter-skelter. Scattered along the bed of the dusty ground were at least a dozen other rock mounds, some bigger and some smaller, but all of them maintained and as uniform as possible.

Billy turned around and looked up at me. He'd known I was there. "You wanna say something?"

I studied the area. "Like what?"

He shrugged. "I don't know. Like 'God bless him' or something."

"God bless him." I walked down the embankment and through the maze of burial mounds, the morbidity of the place making the hairs on my arms stand up. "You make all these?"

He nodded. "They're called cairns. Indians and stuff did them because they didn't have no headstones. That way, people remember them."

"You killed them all?"

He shrugged, looking off in the distance. "Strays."

I shook my head. "I saw you play with that cat two days before you killed it."

He shrugged. "Yeah, so?"

I swept a finger over the cairns: "All of them?" I said it knowing the truth, but hoping he'd found at least some of them already dead. Roadkill, natural causes, whatever.

He nodded; then his eyes met mine, intense in the afternoon sun. "Yep."

"Why?"

"I told you."

"Your dad?"

He nodded.

"This is weird, man."

He stared at me, cocking his head. "Why? You ain't never been to a cemetery?"

"Yeah, but I don't go out of my way to fill them. Sort of tweaked, don't you think?"

He shook his head. "Ain't like killing a person or nothing."

"No, but . . ."

He picked up the shovel, glancing at the sun. "Gotta get back. Pa's going to be home soon, and he'll strap me if he knows I been here." He walked past me then, slinging the shovel over his shoulder and climbing up the wall of the ravine.

My thoughts were jumbled. "He straps you if you come here?"

He turned. "Yep. Says I don't have any business giving animals a funeral. You eat 'em, work 'em, or kill 'em. He says they don't have no souls anyway, so it's a waste of time."

"Then why do you bury them?"

He walked on, shrugging his narrow shoulders. "Feel like it."

I followed. "Answer me a question."

"What?"

"You like killing them?"

I caught up to him.

He bit his lip as he walked, then shook his head. "My ma loved cats."

"Your dad strap you a lot?

He shrugged. "Sometimes."

I lit a smoke. "He ever hit you with his fist?"

He nodded. "Just once. Said he was sorry, too. Lost

his temper. Strap hurts more, though. You never been strapped?"

"No. I think it's wrong."

Billy kicked a rock. "You called the sheriff, didn't you? That's why he came and looked at me."

"No. My dad did. Did the sheriff talk to your dad?"

"No. Pa found out he came by, though."

"Oh, yeah? What happened?"

"Nothin'."

"You didn't get in trouble?"

"Put me in the Can."

"What's the Can?"

"Hall closet."

My stomach squiggled. "He put you in the closet?"

Billy nodded. "Ain't that bad. Don't have to work or nothing, anyway. Dark, though."

"How long were you in there?"

He spit. "Ain't no clock in a closet."

"How long?"

He stopped, pondering the sky for a second. "Don't know. Long enough I slept, then woke up, then slept again. Gotta pee in a jar when that happens."

"Why'd he put you there?"

"You don't talk family business to people. I did."

"You mean the sheriff?"

He didn't say anything for a minute, and we started walking again. He kicked a clod of dirt. "Thanks for the board. I never really said that."

"You're welcome."

"I like doin' tricks."

"Been practicing more?"

"Yep. When Pa's gone."

We walked for a couple of minutes, reached the gate to his backyard, and stopped. He stared at the back of his house. "You ever wish sometimes you were gone?"

I thought about it for a minute. "Where to?"

He shrugged. "I don't know. Just gone."

I took a second, deciding that I didn't want to talk about what I thought he was talking about. "If you could go anywhere, where would you go?"

He kicked a rock. "Dunno. Maybe with my mom." He looked across the fields. "Sometimes, anyhow."

"She just left, huh? One day here, the next day gone, right?"

He nodded. "Pa says she didn't love us."

"I bet she did. You, I mean."

"Pa says she was a whore."

"What do you think?"

He scrunched his nose up. "I don't know what a whore is."

I took a breath. This was out of my league. I was a stupid teenage kid with a mouth, not some shrink. "A whore is . . ." I paused. "Listen, man, I don't think your mom was that. Maybe your dad was just mad because she left, you know? Pissed off and stuff."

He looked at me like I was the biggest idiot on the face of the planet. "You didn't even know her, so how do you know?"

"What was she like?"

"She used to make me peanut butter and jelly sandwiches, and we got ice cream cones sometimes. We'd sit on the back porch with 'em and let the cats lick ice cream from our fingers."

A twitch of that freakiness went through me, but I ignored it. "Well, that means she's not a whore, it means she was a good mom. Get it?"

He looked at me. "Your mom love you?"

I stopped. Here I was, telling this kid to believe something I didn't know that I believed. "Yeah, she did. She loved me."

He nodded. "Ain't no matter now, huh?"

"What doesn't matter now?"

He shrugged. "Well, she's gone, ain't she?"

CHAPTER 15

*T*hree o'clock rolled around and I was on my last fence slat when Miss Mae banged the back screen door shut, signaling she was coming out to make sure I was doing a good job. She looked down the rows of posts, then nodded. "Come on over here, boy."

I did, waggling my tail and lolling my tongue like a puppy looking for a treat.

She pointed a gnarled finger at the second-to-last post. "That don't look straight."

I looked. "It is. You just have crooked eyes."

She narrowed her crooked eyes at me. "You lipping me?"

I smiled. "Nobody ever told you that?"

"You make sure that fence is straight, hear?"

"Will do."

She slipped her hand into her dress, taking out a twenty-dollar bill and handing it to me. "Any decent man has money in his pocket, and you've worked for it. Now go spend it on that girl of yours. She deserves more than you slinking around her house all the time, looking for a kiss."

I tucked the twenty away. "I'm done?"

She nodded. "You done proved yourself. You work till four every day and you'll have a twenty in your pocket to spend as you see fit."

I added the hours. Twenty bucks a day for eight hours of work added up to two-fifty an hour. Now I knew what it meant to be a ditchdigger without a green card, but I'd take what I could get. "Thirty a day?"

She narrowed her eyes again. "You trying to put an old woman in the poorhouse?"

"No, ma'am."

"Twenty-five, then, and not a penny more." She reached in her mysterious dress again and pulled out a wad of cash, peeling off a five for my day's work and handing it to me.

"Ever heard of a bank?"

She scowled. "Don't trust 'em. Mind your business."

"Yes, ma'am." Then I had an idea. "How about we make a deal?"

She furrowed her brow, suspicious. "What kind of deal?"

I pointed behind the shed. "Does that truck back there run?"

"Did the last time I drove it, but that was three years ago."

"How about this. If I can get it running, it's mine through the fall, except I have to do all your errands for you, anytime you want me to. No complaints."

She considered. "I'll do you one better. Same deal, 'cept you get the title to the truck come winter."

"Cool! I'll take it."

"I ain't done."

"Oh. Go ahead."

"You pay me twenty-five dollars a week until that time comes. Then you bought it fair and square."

I smiled, then handed her the five dollars I'd bargained for minutes ago. There was no getting around this woman. Shrewd. "Deal."

"Deal." She took a pack of cigarettes from another part of her dress, then a lighter from yet another part of her dress. I wondered if there was any furniture in there. She lit up. "Your daddy been moping 'round this house all day like he lost his pet fish."

"Yeah."

"Suppose you two still have differences."

"Yes."

"Bet it was hard for you."

"Not easy, that's for sure."

"The hardest things won in this life ain't hard for no reason, Benjamin Campbell."

"He doesn't want to talk about it."

She laughed in that gravelly chicken-gullet laugh, low and quiet. "Suppose there's times there ain't room for talk." She patted me on the shoulder. "Now go get yourself cleaned up. You stink."

My future wife picked me up that night, and we had our first non-working-your-ass-off date. We ate at the burger joint in town, ordering milkshakes for dessert and talking about stuff.

The only other girl I'd *really* dated had been Hailee, and the times we'd gone out had been more party related. We'd both been into the rave scene, and any kind of serious conversation had been hampered by earsplitting music. Then everything crumbled with her mom's overdose, and Hailee was gone. Ben's life, chapter two. Chicks leave.

Kimberly was so totally and completely different than Hailee that it wasn't even funny. She didn't like punk rock, had no desire to do anything wrong or illegal, didn't wear black lipstick, had no piercings or tattoos, didn't smoke or swear, and sitting across from her at the burger joint, I realized I had my hands full on an intellectual level, which suited me about as well as a boil on my ass.

Every time I looked at her mouth when she talked I wanted to stick my tongue in it, and that didn't go well when you actually had to listen to a person speak so you could give an intelligent answer. It also didn't help that every time I pictured her naked breasts, they morphed into Dirk's fists speeding toward my face.

We talked about law school and politics and life in Montana and life in Spokane, and before I realized it, two hours had gone by and I actually found myself wondering if the whole boy-girl conversation thing wasn't all that bad. She asked me what I wanted to do when I got out of school, and she laughed when I told her I wanted to be her house husband and greet her at the door wearing a checkered G-string, with a rose in my mouth. Then I told her I had a compulsive-feelings disorder and that I couldn't seem to control verbal outbursts. She called me a romantic, and I think she liked the sound of it.

We talked about Billy, too. I explained that on the one hand the kid was great, and on the other he was like a Future Serial Killers of America award winner. A moment passed after that, and I studied her. "I want to show you something," I said.

She eyed me warily. "What?"

"Are you busy tonight?"

"What time?"

"Around one?"

"One? In the morning?"

"Yeah."

She looked at her fingers. "My dad would never let me. Not that late."

I shrugged. "Don't tell him."

She frowned. "Ben, I can't."

I frowned back. "I'll be on our back porch at one tonight. Meet me if you want, okay? No strings attached, but I really want you to come."

"To do what?"

I smiled. "It's a mystery."

Just then, Greg Thompson, Kimberly's ex-boyfriend, and Ron Jamison walked in. Greg glanced at us, then turned to the menu board. Ron saw us and came over, sliding into the booth beside Kim. She moved away from him. He smiled, making himself at home. "On a date? Awesome." He called to Greg. "Hey, Greg, come here. I want you to meet my new buddy." He looked at me as Greg came over. "What was your name again? Benald?"

"Sure."

Greg nodded to me, and we shook hands. He looked at Kim. "Hi, Kim."

"Hi, Greg."

Greg looked around uncomfortably. "Come on, Ron. Let's order."

Ron laughed. "What's your hurry, Greg? Come on, sit down and visit."

He didn't sit.

Ron smiled. "Come on, man. Sit. We're all friends, right?" Then he looked at me. "Hey, Benald, how's your little buddy? Showing him some 'moves' on the board?"

Greg cut in before the sparks could fly. "Your dad is opening a restaurant here in town, huh?" He looked at me, and I frowned, wondering if this was a setup. He nodded. "My dad works at the bank. Ms. Pierce is their loan officer."

I relaxed. "Yeah. A steakhouse."

"Cool."

Ron brightened. "Mmmm. Ms. Pierce. Looks good in those skirts, huh, Benald? Bet your dad would love to . . . Oh, forgot. He doesn't like that type, does he?"

Kim interrupted. "Knock it off, Ron."

Ron sat back, splaying his hands wide. "What? Just making conversation." He looked at me. "Your dad is a queer, right?"

I stared at him. "Yes."

"You ever hear them, you know, knockin' the work boots?" He laughed, slapping his fist into his palm.

Greg was silent, ill at ease. Kimberly rolled her eyes. I smiled. "Yeah, as a matter of fact, your dad came over last night and stayed for a while. He walking funny today?"

Ron's smile disappeared.

I took a sip of my milkshake. "He sounded like a woman, actually. Sort of like this squeal thing, you know?"

Ron clenched his teeth, then smiled. "You'd best mind your manners, freak. You don't belong here."

I stared at him. "I've never fit in with dumbshit rednecks like you."

Greg stood, anxious. "Ben, nice meeting you. Come on, Ron."

Ron got up, his eyes locked on mine. Then he smiled. "You take care, Benald. I'm sure we'll meet again."

I smiled. "Say hi to your dad for me."

Then they were gone. I shrugged, watching them walk out the door. "Guess we ruined their dinner."

Kim looked down. "I'm sorry, Ben."

"For what? You didn't do anything."

She shook her head. "Not everybody is like that here."

I blew it off, but my ears burned and my stomach did what it always did when shit happened. Quivered. Not like butterflies, but almost. "Listen, Kim, I'm used to it. Having a gay dad equals hassle."

"Well, I'm still sorry."

I smiled. The last thing I wanted to do was make this an issue. My dad being gay seemed to infiltrate every corner of my life, and I didn't want it here. "Greg seems like a pretty decent guy."

"He is."

"Why'd you break up?"

She looked away. "Things just didn't work out."

"Was he a jerk to you or something?"

"No. I didn't like the people he hung out with."

"Ron?"

"Yes. And his buddy, Cobie Wilson."

Cobie had also been in the Bronco. "The tagalong?"

"Yes."

"Why does Greg hang with them?"

"He and Ron are cousins. They've been together since they were born."

"You can pick your nose, but you can't pick your relatives."

She giggled. "Greg told me once that Ron bugs him sometimes."

"I would bet Ron bugs a lot of people a lot of the time."

"People ignore it. He's the best pitcher the school has had since the sixties."

"Oh, one of those deals."

"Yeah, and his dad is on the town council."

"Oooh. A politician. Even better."

Kim smiled, and a moment of silence passed. "You know it doesn't bother me, right?"

"What doesn't bother you?"

"Your dad. I mean . . ." Her voice trailed away.

I smiled. "Your dad doesn't bother me, either. I mean, him being straight and all."

She laughed, embarrassed. "That was insensitive, wasn't it?"

"No. Just the truth. Believe me, I don't do well around sensitive people. My dad had the wrong kid to have a gay father."

"I didn't mean it that way."

I met her eyes. "See, that's the thing. You know what bugs me more about people? It's not guys like Ron. It's the liars." I twiddled a fry between my fingers. "Somebody somewhere said that you're supposed to act normal around un-normal things, and everybody just sort of agreed. You have to hide it, you know? So you smile and say the things you're supposed to say, even though everybody is thinking the same thing."

She shook her head. "I don't think it's bad, Ben, if that's what you're thinking."

I shrugged. "I don't care who thinks it's bad, Kim. Really. Maybe a couple of years ago I did, but not now." I sat back, tossing the fry on the tray. "I know what we are, and it ain't normal. Especially around here. Dads aren't supposed to be gay, and you know what? I agree with that." I smiled. "It's not like I was walking around in seventh grade wishing my mom would split and my dad's boyfriend would move in."

"I'm sorry. I didn't mean to bring it up."

I smiled at her discomfort. "I'm not a walking basket case about it, if that's what you mean. We have our crap to deal with just like everybody else."

She looked at her reflection in the window next to the booth, silent.

"You're really uncomfortable talking about this, aren't you?" I asked.

"Yes."

"Why?"

"Because." She sighed. "I don't know. It's just . . ."

156

"Weird, right? Let me guess. Your dad has talked to you about it."

She smiled. "Well, yes. But I'm not homophobic. Neither is he."

"Oooh. The homophobic word."

She frowned. "You know, I can't tell if you're having fun with me or being serious. It's like I can't tell where you stand with it."

I smiled, drawling my best John Wayne. "Well, little lady, I don't know where I stand with it, so I guess we have something in common."

She thought for a minute. "Do you prefer not to talk about it?"

"I'd rather not talk at all."

She laughed. "Don't be nasty, Ben Campbell."

"I can't help it. You bring out the animal in me, but every time I dream about it, your brother comes in and pulverizes me."

"Well, we just might have to change that."

The thrill of Ben almost scoring coursed through me. "Meet me tonight, then?"

She shook her head.

"Say not a word, dear lady. You know where I'll be. One o'clock."

At five after one that night, soft footsteps on the drive-way brought a smile to my face. Romance was in the air, but this wasn't about romance. This was about freaky, and I wondered how she'd take it. Kimberly, in deep shadow, appeared from the corner of the house and

157

looked around. I whispered hello. She jumped, and I stood up. "Sorry."

She took a deep breath. "Where are we going?"

"Come on, I'll show you." I took her hand, and a tingle went up my arm as I did. I led her across the backyard, looking up at the sky. The moon was high, and out in the open, the landscape glowed with a bluish tinge. In Paris or Rome or somewhere else, it might have been romantic, but here it was creepy. I opened the back gate and led her into the fields.

She stopped, tugging at my hand. "Where are we going?"

I smiled. "To make wild love under the moon of a beautiful Montana night."

She took her hand from mine, shaking her head.

I took out a cigarette, looked at the back of Miss Mae's house in the distance, then thought better of lighting up. "Kidding. No funny stuff. I promise."

She wasn't convinced. "Ben . . ."

I chuckled, smiling. "What are you worried about? You know you could kick my ass all over the place if you wanted to. I promise. No moves." I held my hand out to her.

She looked at it, then took it. "No funny stuff."

"Not even a grab-ass. Trust me."

She sighed at my lame attempt at humor, but came along. Once we reached the trees before the ravine, she looked back. "I've never snuck out before."

"I know. Nice girls don't do bad stuff."

She looked around. "If my dad finds out . . ."

I smiled. "Sort of exciting, huh?"

158

She squeezed my hand. "Yeah."

"Come on. This'll freak you out."

"What is it?"

"You'll see." I led her to the other side of the trees. The ravine sloped down before us, clear in the moonlight. I stood there for a moment. "Tell me what you see."

She scanned the ravine for a minute or so, then noticed the grayish mounds strewn about. "What are they?"

"Burial mounds."

She gazed at them uncertainly, stepping back. "What does this have to do with anything?"

I nodded, leading her down among them. "It's Billy's cemetery."

She didn't say anything for a long moment, studying the cairns. "What's in them?"

"Cats. He kills them and brings them here."

Her hand tightened around mine, and she took a deep breath. "I want to go home, Ben. Now. This isn't right."

"I don't know *what* it is. Freaky, huh?" I stood in the moonlight, feeling the chill of the air and the death all around me, but the warmth of her hand kept some of it away. "He's messed up, Kim. Really messed up."

She shivered, shaking her head. "Let's go." She slipped her hand from mine and began walking up the slope.

I caught up to her. "What's the matter?"

She turned around, looking down at me. Tears glistened in her eyes under the moonlight. The cemetery spread out below us. "Why would he do this?"

159

"Because he doesn't like to kill them."

"What?"

"His dad makes him do it. Billy loves cats."

She sniffled, looking over at the mounds. "So he buries them?"

"Yeah. Gives them funerals."

She looked at me. "Why are you so interested in him?"

I thought about it. "We're neighbors. I see him a lot, and he's actually a pretty decent kid."

"It's not that."

I lit a cigarette, but she crinkled her nose, so I put it out. "I don't know. His dad, maybe. He rides him so hard, you know? He just wants to be a kid, and that bastard . . . you know he puts him in the closet when he does something wrong?"

"The closet?"

"Yeah." I looked back toward the houses, not visible from this distance, and caught a flicker of movement to the side of us. I turned, but didn't see anything. A chill ran up my spine.

"So that's why you stole his antlers?"

I groaned. "Why is it always assumed it's me? Jeez."

"The whole town is talking. You did it, didn't you?"

I took her hand and we started back. Glancing to the side, I caught another flash of movement, but couldn't pin it down. "I suppose I'm the town outcast already, huh?"

"I can't say it's right, but most people around here weren't too upset about it."

I grinned. "Well, I thought it was a good one."

"So did a lot of people. Including the sheriff. And besides, you saved my uncle. People are still talking about that."

I wasn't used to people talking about me in a good way, and I had nothing to say about it. "Well, the sheriff didn't seem too happy about the antler thing."

She squeezed my hand, lowering her voice. "He couldn't be officially happy, but I heard him talking to my dad about it this morning, and they were laughing. Mr. Hinks is definitely the sour apple of the town, but . . ."

"But it was a prank, Kim, and I'm glad I could be of service." We walked for a minute, the houses materializing out of the darkness as the weirdness of what we'd seen faded. She let go of my hand, and I felt a tension in her. "What's wrong?"

"Nothing."

I knew what it was. "It's the antlers, isn't it?"

She nodded.

"You don't like it?"

"No. I think it's mean. Even to him."

"Come on, Kim, he's a jerk, and it was fun. Don't you ever feel like getting back at someone?"

She shook her head. "You know who that sounds like?"

"Who?"

"Ron Jamison."

That stopped me cold in my tracks. I turned her toward me, taking her hands in mine. "You don't like him at all, do you?"

"No."

"What did he do to you?"

She slumped a little. "I just don't think it's funny, Ben. That's all."

I nodded. "I, Ben Campbell, will never do anything like that again. I promise."

"You're lying, Ben Campbell."

I drew her closer to me. "If there's one thing I *don't* do wrong, it's lie." Then I kissed her, cupping her chin in my hand and bringing her body against mine. Her lips were warm in the chill of the night, and when we broke apart, I inhaled her breath. Pure sweetness, and even better that it had capped off a spooky outing to Billy's graveyard.

She smiled. "Promise?"

"Promise." Then we kissed again.

Five minutes after I'd walked Kim home and snuck back to the house, I hunkered down behind a clump of sagebrush thirty yards beyond the back gate and waited. I'd seen something. That much I knew, and the chill I'd gotten up my spine said it wasn't a dog or a coyote or a polar bear. It had been a person. I'd almost felt the eyes on us.

It had to be Billy. He'd seen me do the antlers, which told me he was an aspiring detective, and I was sure he'd followed us to his cemetery. Probably to see some guy-girl action, for all I knew. Well, turnabout is fair play. He'd get the fright of his life tonight.

Fifteen minutes passed, and my legs were cramping in the chill. The ground was cold, and my breath came in wispy streams of steam. Another five minutes ground by, and I was about to give up when I saw a figure materialize from the stand of shrub pines. With the moonlight cast over the landscape, the figure looked ghostly, and I breathed into the palm of my hand to hide the steam. Closer. I waited. Then, from twenty yards away, I saw him. It wasn't Billy. I held my breath, and as Ron Jamison slunk by, icicles ran through me like daggers.

CHAPTER 16

*T*hings were still tense with Dad, of course, and my course of action was no course of action. Half of me wanted to move out and the other half wanted to hop in his lap and get a big hug from my daddy. With the realization that the former was impossible because I was a loser who made twenty-five bucks a day and that the latter would be plain odd, I avoided him as much as he avoided me.

Then, one morning, the doorbell rang. I was in the kitchen, and Edward answered. Muffled low voices, then Edward came back, cradling his hand. "There is a very large, and I might add very attractive, young man asking for you. Don't shake his hand. He'll break it."

It could only be him. The person of my nightmares, Dirk Johan. Kissing Kim during our romantic sneak-out flashed through my mind. I'd only brushed her teeth with my tongue—no touchies, either—but my testicles shriveled into my stomach. "Tell him I got castrated and joined a eunuch colony."

Edward frowned. "Dear our Lord in heaven, Ben. You didn't . . ."

I smiled, his words reminding me of something Miss Mae would say. Edward might be different, but the fruit didn't fall far from the tree. "Just a kiss, man. I didn't even feel her up. I swear."

He brushed that off with an absent wave of his hand. "Then go. Mother is here. She'll protect you from the goliath."

I stood. "Have a slingshot handy?"

"He's waiting. Don't be rude."

I walked to the front door. Dirk stood on the porch. I stayed inside. "Hi, Dirk."

He looked at me. His arms and chest bulged. He could wear loose-fit jeans and they'd be tight. Square jaw, blue eyes, blond hair—he was like a redneck Viking waiting to plunder my tender flesh. He asked me if I was going to come out.

"Not really. So, what's going on? Collecting for church? Here, I've got some cash on me." I fumbled in my pocket.

"Sis tells me I need to get to know you."

"Me? No. I think we're fine, don't you? I mean, we have a great repertoire, really. You grunt, I smile, all good, huh?"

He smiled, and it might have been a wholesome, full-grain country-boy smile, but I knew better. "I'm going skeet shooting at two. I'll pick you up," he said.

I stared through the screen at him, then realized that finding protection against him behind a screen door was like covering yourself with tinfoil against an atomic blast. "You know, I really appreciate the offer, but . . ."

"Listen, I wanted to thank you for helping out my

uncle. I'll be back. See ya." Then he was gone, trudging down the steps. I walked back to the kitchen in a daze.

Edward sipped coffee. "Going on a date?"

"Ha. I'm going to be the target."

Edward laughed. "Shooting, huh?"

I rolled my eyes. "You heard every word he said. Yes, shooting."

Dad walked into the kitchen. "Shooting?"

Edward nodded. "Dirk, Kimberly Johan's brother, has invited Benjamin to go on a skeet-shooting foray this afternoon."

Dad walked to the sink and filled a glass from the tap. "You've never shot a gun, Ben."

"I don't think I'll be shooting."

He turned. "You're going?"

"Apparently so."

He walked across the kitchen. "Oh." Then he walked out.

I looked at Edward. "What was that all about?"

If Edward was good at one thing, it was deflecting conflict. "Well, Ben, if you are wondering, why don't you go find out?" Then he walked out, too.

I leaned against the counter. Great. Shooting. Guns. Traditional rural life. I wondered if "skeet" was some secret code word for "city people," and I was the only city people here.

Dirk pulled up in a shiny new Ford F-350 pickup truck. It was huge and red. There was a stepladder under the doors to get in. Back in Spokane, it was a joke we had going that all the guys driving around in jacked-up

166

trucks with huge tires were compensating for something, but here it wasn't that way. The storm out at Uncle Morgan's had taught me that. Trucks were utility items here. A necessity.

Dirk honked and I walked out, saying goodbye to Miss Mae, who sat on one of the front-porch rockers. She chuckled. When I got to the passenger door, I reached—at *chest* level, mind you—for the door handle and opened it. "Hi, Dirk." Then I hopped in.

"Howdy."

I shut the door, he put the pickup in gear, and we were off. The truck had all the bells and whistles. CD player, electric everything, outside temp, inside temp, leather interior, and an extra cab with seats behind us. I thought about the truck behind the shed, which I hadn't even had time to look at. "Nice truck."

"Money's good in Wyoming."

"Kim said you bust horses?"

He nodded, steering with his palm while dipping a pinch of tobacco from a can and stuffing it in his front lip.

I had no idea what "busting horses" was, but I could pretend. "Like racehorses?"

He smiled, the pooch in his lip stretching tight. "No. The ranch is the biggest wild horse outfit in the country."

"Oh, so you tame them. Like rodeo stuff."

"Yep. Busting horses."

"Oh."

We drove, and then turned down a gravel road. Dirk goosed the gas, and the big truck's rear end broke loose, spinning us to the side and spitting gravel before he straightened us out. He glanced over at me, noticing my hands clenching the armrest and seat. He chuckled. "Gotta pick up somebody first."

I was in no position to comment, so I looked out the window as the fields passed. Dirk punched a button on the stereo, and some country-singer guy came through, singing about a pink Cadillac. I sort of liked it, and after a few seconds, hummed along. This wasn't that bad, actually. We were high up in a truck that probably cost a billion bucks, the fields sped past, and Pink Cadillac Guy sang his twang over the speakers. I wore my ropers and a regular pair of Levi's with a black T-shirt and a backwards Jeep baseball cap that I'd found at the drugstore. The cowboy hat sat lonely on my dresser.

I bobbed my chin to the music, but not like a dork. This was cool. I could get into this. The longer I lived here, the more I liked the open space. Less people, more sky. Solitude. The attitude wasn't hokey, either. Dirk had it going, I realized. He spit into an empty Pepsi can in the cup holder. "Ever been shooting?"

"No."

He smiled. "Didn't think so. Suppose the only shooting going on in the city is aimed at people."

"Pretty much."

He shook his head, his tone even and friendly. "Get a bunch of people together and they go crazy."

I smiled, adjusting my hat back to frontwards. "I'd agree with you there." He drove and the minutes passed, the truck speeding across the rolling plains. I glanced at the speedometer. Seventy miles per hour on a gravel road. The truck handled like it was on pavement. Smooth as glass.

Ten minutes and several songs later, Dirk told me it was Dwight Yoakam, like that would mean anything to me. We turned down a drive and came up to a ranch house. Dogs barked and ran out to the truck, and a moment later, a man in dusty faded jeans, cowboy hat, ripped T-shirt, and boots came out of a huge garage. He held a wrench, and wiped his hands with a rag. Dirk hopped out, and a dog jumped all around him. Dirk knelt, furiously rubbing the dog's neck and back before standing. I got out and came around the truck. Dirk pumped hands with the guy, who looked around forty. "Good to see you, Dirk. How's your uncle?" the man said.

"Mending." Dirk looked at me. "Ben, meet Colt Holcomb."

Colt nodded to me, then we shook. "Nice to meet you, son. Good job out there with Morgan."

He hadn't called Dirk "son," and we were only two years apart. "Nice to meet you, Colt."

Colt pointed to the dog. "Been a while since he's seen you. Still mopes around sometimes."

Dirk reached down and petted him. "Damn dog is more trouble than he's worth sometimes. Thanks for taking him."

Colt nodded. "Got me a broken axle to fix 'fore tomorrow, boys. We'll be seeing you." He looked at me. "Take care, Ben."

"You, too."

Dirk walked to the bed of the truck and lowered the

gate. "Get on up, Skeet." Then he slapped the gate. The dog bounded up a good three feet, sliding a few inches on the bed liner and wagging his tail.

I stared at the dog. "I don't even want to know."

Dirk screwed his eyes up. "Don't even want to know what?"

"You, like, give him a head start, right?"

"What?"

"The dog. You said we were going to shoot Skeet."

Dirk nodded. "He's been a thorn in my side since the day he was born. Come on."

I got in, and we were driving again. A few minutes passed. I glanced back at the dog standing with his head in the wind. "I don't think I can do this, Dirk."

He shook his head. "Just a dog, Ben. Come on, it'll be fun. You just aim for a leg, then I'll put him down."

"I'm not shooting that dog."

A moment passed, then Dirk busted up laughing. "Damn, you *are* gullible. Skeet are clay pigeons. Little round Frisbee-like things. Skeet is a bird dog, and my best friend. I take him hunting."

I smiled a smile of relief. "Who said I was gullible?"

"Kim. Said you don't know a lot about things."

"Well, when you come to a place with bullet holes in every road sign within a hundred miles, it makes you wonder about life in general."

He laughed. "Had him since I was fourteen. He's like my little bro."

"You couldn't take him to Wyoming?"

"Nope. Colt hunts more than Dad. Kept him up on it for me." Dirk drove back down the road for ten more minutes, then hung a right on a narrow, rutted path. We came to a clearing with a stand of tall bushes on the far side and he stopped.

I got out, and Dirk opened the extra cab door on his side, bringing out two long cases. Skeet hopped over the bed wall and promptly began sniffing around. Dirk tucked one of the cases under his arm and lowered the tailgate, then set the cases down. "Hey, grab those shells from your side, huh?"

I opened the rear door on my side and found five boxes of shells. "These are the bullets, then?"

Dirk spit, then unlatched one of the cases. "Shells, not bullets. Rifles shoot bullets. Shotguns shoot shells."

"Oh. Thanks." I brought the boxes to the tailgate and set them down.

Dirk laughed, then proceeded to take a humongous weapon out of the first case. "So, Sis tells me you're afraid of me."

I stared at him holding the gun. Why pretend? "Yeah."

He smiled. "That ain't a bad thing, I suppose."

I eyed the gun. "Kim will be mad if you kill me."

He laughed. "I ain't going to kill you, little man. Fact is, I think I like you. Her last boyfriend wouldn't even look at me."

"Greg?"

He shrugged. "Some such name as that. Met him when I visited from Wyoming last year."

"I thought everybody knew each other here."

He glanced at me, then checked the shotgun. "I've been gone four years. Dropped out of school when I was fifteen and took off."

"You dropped out?"

"School ain't for me. Money to be made, and I make it. Been the ranch manager for two years." He held the shotgun out to me. "Browning, limited edition. Don't drop it."

I stared at it.

"Take it. Watch the barrel—don't put your finger on the trigger."

I took it. It was lighter than I thought it would be. Dirk gave me a quick lesson on how it worked. Breech, action, how to hold it, how to load it, unload it, how to shoot it, always know where the barrel is pointing, never put your finger on the trigger until you're ready to fire. Dirk handed me a pair of earmuffs and put a pair on himself. I put mine on and everything was muffled.

Then he took out a spring-loaded contraption on a tripod and set it up, taking a big box of skeet from the truck and setting it at the side. The skeet shooter, he said. Then he loaded it. I set down the shotgun and he showed me how to use the shooter thing, then picked up his own shotgun. "When I say 'pull,' you push that lever," he said.

"What about the dog?"

"Bird dog. He'll mind himself."

He loaded his shotgun and put it to his shoulder. "Pull!"

I pushed the lever, the spring unloaded, and the skeet flew into the air at an angle. The barrel of Dirk's shotgun followed it for two seconds before a boom echoed across the fields. The clay pigeon exploded into dust. I gawked. "Damn!"

He smiled, opening the breech and expelling a smoking shell. "Lead it just a little bit. I set the choke wide on yours, so the spread will be pretty good."

He set his shotgun down, then helped me load mine, putting it on safety. He took his position at my side, getting ready to click the latch. I snugged the shotgun to my shoulder and aimed into the sky, sliding my finger into the trigger guard after I released the safety. "Pull!"

The spring sprung and the skeet flew. I led it, then pulled the trigger. The kick rocked me back, and it wasn't a little kick. It was an almost-fell-on-my-ass kick, and I felt like my shoulder was dislocated. Dirk stood by the skeet machine. "Almost. A little behind."

I held the shotgun, unable to rub my pounding shoulder. I would not admit pain in front of this person. "Let me try again."

Dirk nodded. "Load her up. The red shells."

I did so, then clenched my teeth as I snugged the stock once again into my shoulder. "Pull!" This time I didn't almost fall, but the pain in my shoulder doubled. I'd missed. I breathed deep. "Again."

And so it went. I took seven more shots, and on the last, I chipped the skeet, sending it wobbling into the brush. Victory at last. My shoulder felt like it was going to fall off. "Here, Dirk, you go."

We shot for another hour, Dirk hitting thirty out of thirty-two and me hitting three out of twenty. By the time we loaded up the truck, I felt like weeping. The pain in my shoulder had gone from a centralized place to the entire right side of my upper body, my right arm, and my neck. I needed a shot of morphine. Instead, Dirk sat on the tailgate, popped a small cooler open, and handed me a can of beer. I drank half of it simply to ease the pain. He smiled. "Did okay for the first time."

I didn't understand it. He'd taken twice as many shots as I had and I'd watched his face. He hadn't even winced. I decided skeet shooting was a sport that would be great if it didn't hurt so much. "Thanks."

"Going bird-hunting next week. Interested?"

I sighed inside. "Sure."

He pointed at me with his beer. "Shoulder hurt?"

"Naw."

He laughed. "Good deal." He finished his beer, crumpled the can, then threw it in the bed of the truck. "Let's go."

Two hours later, after a hot bath and dinner in my room because I didn't want to be around Dad, my shoulder was already turning purple. I lay on my bed when Edward knocked. *Entrez.*

Edward came in, holding the phone. "For you."

I took it with my left hand, since my right arm wouldn't really move. "Hello?"

"Hi."

"Hey, Kim."

She cleared her throat. "Are you okay?"

"Why wouldn't I be okay?"

"Because of my brother."

I frowned into the phone. "I had a great time. Shot some skeet, you know? I got a few, too."

"He told me." Then she paused. "Ben, I've got to

apologize to you. I'm totally mad at Dirk for what he did, and I had no idea."

"What?"

"He gave you a box of double-aught magnums to shoot with. I'm sorry."

"What does that mean?"

"It means that what you were shooting was over twice as powerful as what he was shooting. It's also why you only hit a few. There's only two lead slugs in each shell, as opposed to around fifty or sixty small ones in his." She paused. "I'm surprised your shoulder isn't broken."

I groaned. Now I knew why Dirk had laughed after he asked me if my shoulder hurt.

She was hopping mad. "He thought it was a good joke. You know, breaking the kid into shooting. I could kill him."

I smiled. It was a good joke. "Paybacks are a bitch."

"Are you okay?"

"Besides not being able to move my shoulder, I'm perfect. Wanna arm-wrestle?"

"No, but he'll apologize when you see him next. I told him he had to."

I laughed. "Hey, I took it like a man, didn't I?"

She laughed this time. "He said you actually did okay. He was surprised you went on for as long as you did."

After we hung up, I oozed farther into the bed, the only working part of my body, unfortunately, my brain. I thought about Kim and Dirk and Uncle Morgan and all the things that had happened in this Podunk town so far, and then, Ron Jamison sprung into my head.

Why had he followed me and Kim? To me, it went beyond the smart-ass townie giving the new kid a hard time. It went into the creepy and weird. What was he doing? Had he planned on scaring us for a good "boo!" but decided not to? Then I wondered how he knew we had plans to meet at one in the morning. Not exactly a common hour for him to be walking by and seeing us sneak out, that was for sure.

I decided there was a possibility that somebody in the hamburger joint had heard me ask Kim to meet and they'd told Ron the plan. I hoped it was that, and nothing more than Ron Jamison having a major malfunction with me.

CHAPTER 17

*T*he next day went by with the misery of my shoulder reminding me that Dirk Johan was a very evil and mean country boy. I popped ibuprofen all day long as I worked on the fence, and by midmorning I'd actually stretched out enough to function. Besides being bruised, it wasn't that bad.

After lunch, Edward and Dad came out the back door and hopped in the minivan, with Edward calling that they were going to some town or another to look at restaurant furniture. Dad said nothing, just got in and fired up the car, and they pulled away.

Then Miss Mae came out. "Ben!"

I turned, two nails in my mouth and the hammer in my hand. "Yesh?"

"I need bacon. Three pounds'll do."

I looked back at the fence. "I . . ."

"We had a deal. You'd do errands for me."

I spit the nails into my hand. "I haven't even gotten the truck going. That's not fair."

"Deal is a deal, and I don't remember you saying it started when you got the darn thing going. Get on to the butcher shop and put it on account. And get me one of those lemon pies I like. The little ones. I've got a craving."

I sighed. "Fine, I've got to get more nails, too."

"Go to the hardware store and tell Mrs. Gunderson to put that on account as well."

I set the hammer on the table, took off my work belt, and walked down the driveway as Miss Mae marched back into the house. Fifteen minutes later I was at the hardware store, weighing out two pounds of nails, when I heard a familiar voice behind me. "Getting everything all right?"

I turned, and Greg stood there. He wore an apron with "GUNDERSON'S HARDWARE, TACK AND FEED" emblazoned on it. "Hey. I didn't know you worked here."

He shrugged. "Part-time, summers. My aunt and uncle own it."

"Cool."

"Puts gas in the Beast and gets me around, anyway."

"Your Bronco?"

"Yeah. Mr. Hinks set up a deal for me last summer at an auction in Big Springs. Breaks down like clockwork. This week it was the alternator."

"That sucks."

He glanced at the nails. "Building something?"

"Fence. I've become Miss Mae's work slave since we got here."

He laughed. "I know the feeling. She hired me last year to rototill her garden. After the third time, she decided I'd done it right."

"Her bark is worse than her bite. She's nice as long

as you do things her way." I held up the bag of nails. "I'd better get back. I've got to figure out how to get her truck running later, but I've got to get that fence finished."

"That Chevy in the back?"

"Yeah." I explained our deal.

"Work on engines much?"

"No. Figured I'd pop the hood and start wiggling things."

He hesitated. "I'm off at four. Need a hand?"

I adjusted my hat, wondering if this would turn into some "get the new guy" trap. But I was absolutely brain-dead when it came to mechanics. "Sure."

"Cool. I'll come over."

When I got back, I set the bacon and the lemon pie on the kitchen counter and lugged myself to the fence. My shoulder had tightened up while I was gone, and I worked the kinks out for another couple of hours, until four rolled around.

I cleaned up, then went out back, taking five minutes to figure out how to pop the hood. I at least wanted to make it look like I knew something other than turning the ignition. The keys sat on the dash. I jammed one in the keyhole and turned it. Nothing. Not even a click.

I got out of the cab and sat on a stump, smoking a cigarette. I'd decided to quit smoking because Kim didn't like it, but it was turning out to be a hard thing to do. A few minutes later, Miss Mae banged out the back screen and hollered, "You got a visitor!"

I stood, walking to the back door as Greg came out. I led him to the truck. "Thanks for coming," I said.

He carried a toolbox in one hand and a battery in the other. "No problem. I like working on 'em when I don't have to buy the parts."

I pointed to the battery. "What's that for?"

"That truck has been sitting there for over two years. The battery is shot. Guaranteed."

"How much do I owe you for it?"

"Nothing. I just got a new one for the Beast. This one'll do you for a bit."

"Cool."

He opened his toolbox and took out a wrench, bending over the grille and taking the old battery out. I lifted the battery he'd brought and set it next to him. He put it in. "See, the red wire is always hot; black is the ground. Get 'em mixed up and you'll blow the alternator."

Greg finished connecting the wires and told me to get in and crank it. I did, and the engine turned over, grinding several times before he signaled me to stop. I hopped out. He bent under the hood again. "Fuel filter is probably gunked up."

Fifteen minutes and some small talk later, Greg had a small cylindrical thing in his hands. It had two holes, one on either end. He put one end to his lips and blew. It barely gurgled. "Plugged. Not all the way, though."

"We need a new one?"

"Naw. We can clean it." He took a spray can out of his toolbox and sprayed into either end, then plugged the holes and shook. He set the filter down. "We'll let it sit for a few, then wash it out with gas." He looked around. "Got a can around here somewhere?"

"Yeah. I'll get it." I went to the shed, grabbed the mower can, and brought it back. Greg sat on the stump and put a chew in his lip. "You like it here?"

"Sure. It's not that bad."

He looked at me. "Kim's a nice girl."

"Yeah."

He shook his head. "I don't have a beef with that. Just wanted to be clear on it, is all. It was nothing serious between us, anyway."

I definitely didn't want to talk about it. "Cool." Just then, we heard somebody coming down the driveway, whistling. "Hey, Greg!" he called.

Greg sighed, then stood up, calling to the whistler, "Yeah, Ron! Back here."

Ron appeared around the side of the shed a moment later. He looked at us, then smiled. "Looky here. We got some engine work going on?"

Greg picked up the gas filter and shook it. "Yeah. Getting this thing running." He sprayed more stuff in it.

Ron nodded. "Hey, Ben. How's it hangin'?"

"Hey, Ron."

Greg flushed the filter with gas several times. "How'd you know I was here?" he asked.

Ron smiled. "Eyes and ears everywhere, cousin. Your mom told me."

I watched as Greg blew through the cylinder again. This time it whistled. He spit gas residue from his lips. "Should be good, Ben."

I stepped forward. "Here, I can get it. I saw how you took it off." He handed the filter to me, and I bent to it.

Ron made a clicking noise with his cheek. "So'd the old lady give this clunker to you, Ben?"

I struggled with the gas lines, soaking my hands and the ground. "No. I bought it. Or am buying it."

He laughed. "That's one A-list bitch you got in there, that's for sure. She wouldn't give a knob job to a wood-pecker on a cold winter's day."

Greg interrupted. "Ron, come on. Knock it off."

"Dude, just saying. Calm down, man. I didn't mean anything by it."

I talked from under the hood. "She can be that way."

Ron laughed. "For sure, man."

I laughed, and it wasn't in a jovial way. "She doesn't like you."

He smirked. "See, that's the thing. What's not to like about me? I'm the nicest guy around."

I thought about the cemetery. "Greg, these clamps just go on like this, right?"

Greg looked under the hood. "Yeah. We'll make sure they don't leak when we get it fired up."

Ron was on a roll. "You guys look sort of cute to-gether under there. Might make a good couple. You think, Greg?"

Greg ignored him.

I wiped my hands with a rag, then threw the gasoline-soaked thing at Ron. He caught it reflexively, and I smiled. "Thanks."

Then he dropped it, wiping his hands on the ground, his eyes flint. "Sure, man. Anytime. So, I heard you lopped off Weirdo's antlers."

I shrugged. "That's the thing with rumors. Never know what the truth is."

Ron hooted, slapping his leg. "For sure, Benald. Man, that kind of shit is right up my alley. Wish I thought of it first."

Greg checked the spark plug wires, asking Ron what he'd come by for. Ron made that sound with his cheek. It reminded me of what old men did when they winked at you. "Just thought I'd drop on by the house to see what you were up to, and your mom told me where you were. There's a party at the Pond tonight."

Greg struggled with a wire. "Busy. Sorry."

Ron frowned. "Come on, Greg. You always used to want to do shit, and now you're like some dork or something. Lighten up."

Greg straightened, wiping his hands on another rag. He looked at his cousin, and his expression wasn't necessarily friendly. Then he shrugged. "I'm busy."

"No prob, man." He turned to me, smiling. "Hey, Benald, you want to come? Have a few beers and meet some people?"

I turned away, grabbing a wrench and checking the battery cables for no reason. I couldn't tell if he was making a peace offering or setting me up. "I'll think about it."

Ron made to go. "Cool. Lame-ass here can tell you where it is, if you're so inclined to join us. Adios."

A few minutes after Ron left, Greg finished up checking what he called the "points" under the distributor cap. "Okay, we'll give it a shot."

"What's his deal?"

"Ron?"

"Yeah."

"He's okay. He just gets a mouth on him some-times."

"Obviously."

Greg shook his head. "He was pissed because of the Ronald comment you made when you first met. He hates being called that. That's why he was a jerk at the diner."

"Guess he can dish it . . ."

Greg laughed. "But can't take it. That would be Ron. Once you get to know him, he's decent."

I wasn't so sure about that. Something bugged me about him, and it wasn't just the cemetery. The way his eyes slid over things. Especially Kim. "Why aren't you going to the party tonight?"

Greg shrugged. "I don't know. Same old same old. Drink too much, sick all the next day. It gets stupid af-ter a while."

I nodded. I could understand that. "Should I hop in and try it?" I asked. Greg gave the affirmative on that, and I did so. I pumped the gas a few times and turned the key, listening to the engine struggle. Greg leaned over the grille and sprayed some stuff into the carbure-tor, and the engine fired up. I gave it gas and it bellowed smoke. I grinned. "Awesome!"

He came around to the driver's door, all business. "Let it run for a second. The carb needs to burn the gunk out. It'll stop smoking in a few minutes."

I hopped out and helped Greg pack his tools. "Thanks, man. I appreciate it."

He picked up his toolbox. "Sure. Anytime."

I was excited. The truck rumbled behind me as Greg walked to the driveway. Then he turned. "Hey, Ben?"

"Yeah?"

"Don't go to that party tonight, huh?"

I looked at him, trying to read what he was saying. "Sure. No problem."

CHAPTER 18

*T*he next day, I had a visitor.

"She says I should say 'sorry.' "

I looked at Dirk, standing there with his hands in his pockets at our front door. I laughed. Kim stood at the curb, glaring at her brother's back. "Dude, no problem. You got me."

"She's been making my life pure hell for two days."

"I'll bet." I waved to her. She waved back, but the glare didn't leave.

"We do that to new guys. You know, initiation."

"Understood, Dirk. I still had a good time."

He looked at me. "You up for bird-hunting? No tricks. I promise."

"Did she make you invite me?"

He smiled. "Hell, no. She can do just about anything but get in the way of bagging birds." He shuffled. "I figured I owed you for the other day."

I thought about it. "Sure."

"I'll drop by. Thursday morning. Five o'clock."

"Sounds cool. See ya."

When Dirk had gone, Kim came to the door. I kissed her. "Hey, lady. You didn't have to do that."

"I know. I wanted to."

"I got my truck running yesterday. Wanna go cruising tonight? We can make out under the stars."

She brightened. "No, but my dad wants you over."

"Your dad?"

"Yes. For dinner."

"Tonight?"

"Don't tell me you had plans?"

I smiled. "No. Sure, that sounds fine."

"Don't worry. Dirk is staying out at Uncle Morgan's now. I made him come to town to apologize."

"Wow, you do have some power."

She giggled. "Don't cross me, Ben Campbell, or you'll find out, too." She kissed me. "Five-thirty. Don't be late." Then she was gone and I was watching her hips move down the walk. I'd kissed the lips connected to that butt. Awesome.

I turned around and Dad was standing there. "Quite the social calendar you've got going."

"Yeah."

"Things getting serious with Kim?"

"I don't know."

"You're going hunting?"

"Yes. Got a problem with that?"

"You've never been hunting."

"When in Rome." I looked at him, using his words: "People do things differently here, right?"

He looked at me. "I don't like this, Ben."

I turned and walked up the stairs. Hell, I didn't know what he was talking about. Probably hunting and every-thing between him and me and how he felt about it, but I wasn't interested. I'd found something I felt like I was finally fitting into, and he could accept it or not. Just like he'd told me: "Deal with it."

I knocked on Kim's door at five-thirty sharp, after Miss Mae looked me over and made me go change my shirt. "I'll have no slouch representing my family."

I changed, and she approved. "Better. Now mind your manners and have a good time."

Then I did something I never thought I'd do. I kissed her cheek. "I will." Then I was gone. I didn't walk, though. I drove. Four houses. Because I could. Mrs. Johan answered the door. I hadn't talked to her but a few times out at the Morgan farm, and she seemed nice. Round-cheeked and plump, she had the same blue eyes as the rest of her family, and she wore dresses just like Miss Mae, but a little bit more modern. "Hello, Benjamin. Come in."

I did, and saw Mr. Johan sitting in a recliner, read-ing the paper. Mrs. Johan went to the kitchen. He nodded. "Ben."

"Hi, Mr. Johan."

He smiled. "How's the shoulder?"

"Fine, thank you."

He turned a page of the paper. "I can't say it's right, but so goes it with young men."

He sounded just like Kim did when she told me she didn't like the antler joke. "It's fine, really."

"Kim is upstairs. Second door on the right." He

glanced at me over his reading glasses. "You can keep the door open."

I walked up, then knocked. Kim answered: "Hi. Come on in."

I entered the treasured room, leaving the door open as instructed. This was the place where she wore soft underthings around. The place she lay her goddess-like body down to slumber. I glanced at her bed, a four-poster set high. The comforter had daisies printed on it. "Nice room."

She kissed me, then sat cross-legged on the bed. She wore a tight white tank top and sweats. Her hair was in a ponytail. I pried my gaze away from her chest. She smirked. "Behave."

"I didn't even say anything."

"You don't have to. Come here." She patted the bed next to her.

I was on hallowed ground. I felt like sprawling on it and burying my face in the fluffiness just to smell her. I nodded. "I'm really nervous right now."

She slapped my knee. "Why?"

"Because I'm in your bedroom." I flopped back, staring at the ceiling. "And I'm about to go through The Test with your parents."

She flopped back next to me, her arms splayed out. Her right hand rested on my thigh. "The Test?"

I liked the feel of her hand on my leg. "Yeah. The Test."

"Explain."

"You know, to find out what kind of guy is dating their daughter. The Test."

"Oh. Well, just don't pick your nose or something."

"I won't." We stared at the ceiling. "Greg helped me fix the truck."

"He's a good guy."

"Yeah." I glanced over at her. I could smell her body lotion. Vanilla. "Ron came over."

Silence for a moment. "How'd it go?"

"Fine."

"Do me a favor, huh?"

"Name it."

"Just stay away from him."

I thought about what Greg had advised about the party. "Why?"

She rolled into my side, resting her hand on my chest and kissing my neck. "Because I asked you to," she breathed.

I turned my head and she lifted her chin. I kissed her. "Anything you say, dear." Then we kissed again, and kept on kissing. Suddenly somebody cleared his throat. I bolted upright. Mr. Johan stood at the door with a look on his face that said he hadn't wanted to see what he'd seen any more than I'd wanted him to see it. "Dinner's on, kids. Come on down." Then he was gone.

I sighed. "Great."

Kim giggled. "He knows I kiss, Ben."

"Yeah, but it's like watching a porno with your mom. Doesn't quite work, you know?"

Her eyes widened. "You've seen a porno?"

"No," I lied. Of course I'd seen a porno, but I wasn't going to say that. This was rural life.

She lowered her voice, and a wicked smile came to her face. "I did. Just once, though. With Franny Madison during a sleepover in ninth grade."

"Franny the porno freak? I've heard of her."

She laughed. "No, her mom and dad had it. Like from the eighties or something. She stole it."

"Bad girls." I grinned. "I like bad girls."

She stood. "Hey, don't get any ideas. It was sort of gross. But funny. They had, like, this voice-over on it. It didn't match. Franny and I laughed our butts off."

"Okay, fine. I saw one once, too. Same deal."

An uneasy silence came between us, like we were both thinking about something we shouldn't talk about. "Come on, let's eat," she said.

Dinner consisted of baked pork chops, pork gravy, homemade biscuits with honey, green beans, and wild rice. I sat like a little boy at the big people's table. They said the blessing, just like we did at Miss Mae's. "This is delicious, Mrs. Johan."

She smiled. "Thank you, Ben. The biscuits are my grandmother's recipe."

Mr. Johan asked for the honey. I handed it to him. He dribbled some on one. "So, Ben, tell us about Spokane."

I glanced at Kim. We'd talked about the trouble I'd been in, but I somehow didn't think that topic was appropriate. "Well, it's pretty cool."

Mrs. Johan dabbed at her mouth. "What kind of hobbies were you interested in?"

I paused, checking the list. Running from the cops, not good. Smoking pot, not good. Raves, not good. "Um, skateboarding. I skated a lot."

She smiled. "Like on television? I've seen those *Z* games they have."

"*X Games.* Yeah, sort of like that."

Mr. Johan cut in. "So, what kind of grades did you have, Ben?"

"Pretty good. Could have been better, I guess, but I got sidetracked."

"Oh?"

"Yeah. My mom leaving and everything. I lost interest for a while."

He smiled, and it was sincere. "Understandable. Any plans for the future?"

Here comes the Ben I can't control. The Ben that comes in spasms. "Well, I figured I'd finish school, get a job, buy a place, and marry your daughter."

Silence. Utter and complete silence. Then Kim laughed, embarrassed. "Ben . . ."

I shrugged. "Sorry. Can't help it. These are great biscuits, Mrs. Johan. Pass the butter?"

Later on, as I lay in my bed, I thought of Kim. I could still smell her. I could still feel her hand on my leg. I fell asleep smothered in her.

CHAPTER 19

*T*hen all hell broke loose. I woke up the next morning to the sound of Mr. Hinks and my dad yelling at each other. It wasn't pretty. I heard it all the way upstairs. I scrambled out of bed and into my clothes, listening to the voices. I'd never heard my dad yell before. Ever. He'd never even gotten into an argument over a parking space, let alone a yelling match with a car auctioneer, and my heart thumped in my chest. I ran out of my room and then slowed, padding down the stairs.

They were out on the front porch. Edward was watching them from the middle of the living room, and when he saw me coming down the stairs, he shook his head and pointed, signaling me to go back up. But I didn't.

Then the yelling stopped, and the thud and clunk and crash of struggling bodies shook the house. I turned the corner at the base of the stairs just as Edward bolted to the screen door, and there I saw it. My dad and Mr. Hinks were fighting on the porch. A chair had been knocked over, and they grappled standing up, trying to pin each other to the railing.

My dad had a hold of Mr. Hinks's upper arms, and

as they struggled against the railing, Edward burst out the door and flung himself between them. Mr. Hinks, with blood dribbling down a swollen lip, braced himself in front of Dad and Edward. His face contorted in rage, he pointed a finger at Dad. "Keep your son off my property, you sonofabitch!" Then he strode down the stairs and walked away.

I watched as Edward comforted Dad, who was breathing heavily and staring at his feet, wiping his mouth with the back of his hand. It came away bloody. Dad said something softly to Edward and shook his head. Edward nodded and came inside. I stood by the stairs. "What happened?"

Edward stopped, staring ice into me. "Well, your father just got into a fistfight because you decided to play the game. I think you should go upstairs now." Then he was gone, heading to the kitchen to get a damp towel.

I had no idea what he was talking about, so I stood there. Edward came back, and as he passed, he told me again to go upstairs, this time in a more conciliatory way. I went.

Lying on my bed, I didn't know who would come up those stairs—Miss Mae, Edward, or Dad himself. I doubted Dad would come. He'd said three sentences to me in as many days. Edward had said I "played the game." What game?

An hour later, I got up and went downstairs. I wasn't going to sit up there waiting all day. I had to know. Dad and Edward stood across from each other in the kitchen, leaning against the counters and talking.

They stopped when I came in. Dad's nose was puffy. I crossed my arms, unsure of what would come next. "What happened?"

Dad walked across the kitchen and faced me, his eyes intense and his voice full of trouble. "Did you do it?"

I stared. "Do what?"

"You put ten decomposed cat carcasses on his front porch last night, then slashed his tires." It wasn't a question.

I shook my head. "No. I didn't. I didn't do anything."

Silence filled the room, and Dad studied my face for a long moment, searching for something. His jaw muscles clenched. "I don't believe you," he said. Then he turned and walked out.

I stood, stunned, then looked at Edward. "I didn't do it, Edward. I swear."

The look on Edward's face said that he didn't know what to believe.

"I didn't do it."

"I don't know what to tell you, Ben."

"Well, tell him I didn't do it!"

Edward sniffed, then shook his head. "No."

My mind reeled. "What happened, then? How'd they get into a fight?"

"Mr. Hinks threatened you."

"Yeah, so? He obviously thinks I did it, and so does everybody else. Big deal."

"No, Ben, it is a big deal."

"Why?"

"Because your dad defended you, that's why. Even though he thinks you did it."

"What, let me guess. Mr. Hinks hit him, so they scuffled."

"No. Your dad told Mr. Hinks he'd have to go through him first if he ever tried to hurt you."

That stopped me. "He said that?"

"Yes. Then Mr. Hinks tried to get past him through the door, so your father hit him."

That stopped me, too. My dad, the guy who followed all the rules, hit *him*? "It wasn't me, Edward."

"Tell that to him, then."

Dad sat on the front porch, and as I walked outside, I didn't even look at him, just kept going. Straight to Mr. Hinks's front door. I knocked hard three times, and a moment later Mr. Hinks answered. I didn't give him time to talk. "I stole your antlers and hid them in my closet. I did it because you strapped Billy for something you knew wasn't his fault. But I haven't done anything else to you or your house, including the cats and your car. So if you want to call the sheriff and have me arrested, or come out here and beat the shit out of me, go ahead. But if you fuck with my dad again, I'll kill you."

Mr. Hinks studied my face for a moment, his own a slab of rock. "Get out of my sight." Then he slammed the door in my face.

Dad stood at the porch rail as I walked across the lawn. Concern flashed across his face. "What are you doing, Ben?" he asked.

I kept going. "Making things right."

Twenty minutes later, I had the pile of antlers out of my closet and had just gotten them carefully stacked in the Hinkses' driveway when the sheriff pulled up. He got out, walked up the drive, and planted his hands on his hips, studying the antlers. "Funny how things just start showing up sometimes."

I sorted the last of the horns. "Arrest me if you want, but let me do this first."

He scratched his ear, then glanced at the slashed tires. "Mind coming clean with me about this whole thing, Ben?"

I straightened. "Sure. I took the antlers, hid them in my closet, and now I'm putting them back. I did it because you and my dad and everybody else in this stinking town doesn't give a crap about Billy Hinks."

He nodded, soaking it in. "The tires?"

I shook my head. "No. But I know who did."

"And I suppose you're not going to tell me?"

"No, I'm not."

He thought about this, glanced at the tires, then eyed me. "I've been hearing a whisper about a young man around here that might not like you too much. Now, taking into consideration what I know about this individual and how he operates, you might want to tell me about it?"

I shrugged. Nothing was a secret around here. "I'm saying I didn't slash Mr. Hinks's tires or do the cats, and I don't really care who thinks I did."

A moment passed. He nodded at the antlers. "Okay, then. Looks like you've got some work to do."

"You're not going to arrest me for these?" I said, pointing to the antlers.

He shook his head. "Looks like you're taking care of it just fine. I'll deal with Mr. Hinks about it." Then he turned. On the way to his Blazer, he knelt by Mr. Hinks's car, examining the slashes. After a moment, he straightened up and left.

I got our ladder and climbed up it, attaching each antler to the garage wall. It took me almost two hours, and every once in a while, I caught a glimpse of Mr. Hinks looking out through the shades.

When I'd finished, I walked inside. Dad had gone with Edward to the bank to sign papers. I grabbed my keys and drove to town. I found Dad and Edward sitting at Ms. Pierce's desk, talking over the loans. I ignored her. Dad and Edward turned when I approached, and it all came out in a burst. "I might be the shittiest son in the world, but I've never lied to you about anything. Not once. That's something you can't say about yourself." Then I strode out, pissed at how I felt about myself and even more pissed at the world that made me feel that way.

On my way home, I thought about what had happened. The cats. Ron Jamison telling me he wished he'd thought about doing the antlers. Greg telling me not to go to the party. Kim telling me to stay away from Ron. Seeing him at the cemetery. It added up.

I'd been set up.

When I got home, I headed out back, hopping the wire fence and walking across the fields. I knew what I'd find. I knew what had happened. Ron Jamison had dug up the cats and dumped them on the porch. He'd done it knowing I'd be blamed.

I jogged the last bit, through the stand of pines and to the edge of the ravine. Ten dug-up graves, the rock cairns scattered all about, greeted me. My stomach sunk. Damn. There was more to Ron Jamison than I knew. Then a rock hit me on the side of the head.

I ducked, then turned, my head hurting like a son-ofabitch. I expected to see Ron, smiling wickedly and winding up for another throw. He wasn't there, though. Billy was.

Billy threw another rock, barely missing me, and I faced him. Tears welled in his eyes. "Dirty bastard!" he cried. He threw again, and I ducked. The rock grazed my shoulder.

"Hey! Stop, Billy!"

Billy's face contorted and tears streamed down his dirty cheeks as he hurled rock after rock at me. "Why'd you do it, huh? Why'd you have to go and do that?"

"I didn't! I swear, Billy, I didn't. I never would."

"Liar!" He threw another one, and it hit me square in the side.

I rushed him, then, and tackled him to the ground. He struggled, but I'd pinned him down. He was stronger than I thought. I looked down at his face, dirty and wet and hysterical. "Knock it off, man! I didn't do this, Billy. I didn't. But I know who did, and I'll take care of it."

He struggled for a minute more, then went totally limp. I rolled away from him and we both lay there, staring at the sky. White heat rose around us. "I know why this means so much to you."

He didn't say anything.

"If there was one thing in the whole world that could happen in your life, what would it be?"

He stared at the sky, bringing an arm up to wipe his face. "That my mom would come get me."

I closed my eyes then, and wished I could feel the same as he did. I didn't, though. My mom was better off being away. "I'll find her for you."

He sat up. "Pa says she fell flat off the face of the earth. Just disappeared. He says people do that when they don't love nobody."

"I think people do things for a lot of different reasons. That's what I think."

"She wouldn't a left if she loved me."

"Maybe she felt trapped. Like she couldn't do anything else. Maybe she was afraid."

He didn't say anything.

"You've never been afraid?"

"Sure. Everybody gets afraid."

I nodded. "Well, when some people get afraid, they run away."

"Maybe so."

"Did your mom ever tell you where her favorite place was?"

"She told me once she'd like to take me to Las Vegas. We was looking through a magazine and she showed me. All lights and glittery stuff everywhere. They got a big pirate boat there that sinks. Pirates jumping in the water and cannons goin' off. I like pirates."

"Cool."

Billy thought about something for a moment. "I

ain't killin' cats no more. My dad can do it if he wants."
He picked up a rock and threw it. "I'm gonna be a vegetarian."

"A vegetarian?"

"Yeah. When I grow up. Then I can help them."

"You mean a veterinarian?"

"Yeah. The guy that makes animals better."

I smiled. "I think you'd make a good one."

CHAPTER 20

*T*hursday morning. Bird-hunting. The closest thing I had to camouflage gear were my long camo skater shorts and a wheat-colored T-shirt. It'd have to do. As I wiped the sleep out of my eyes and went downstairs, Miss Mae called from the kitchen. I walked in. "Morning."

She didn't turn from the sink. "Morning."

"I'm going bird-hunting."

She nodded, pointing to the counter. "Lunch and a thermos of coffee for you."

I smiled. "Thanks."

She busied herself with buttering two slices of toast, then brought me a plate of scrambled eggs with them. "You've got work today."

I dug into my breakfast. "I'll make it up, okay?"

"You put dinner on the table and that's your work." Then she walked out of the kitchen, leaving me to eat alone. Eat birds? I didn't think we were hunting chickens. I wolfed down the rest of my eggs and toast, then eyed the thermos of coffee. After a moment of thinking, I got up and grabbed my stuff, stopping off in the bathroom before I hit the door and waited on the porch.

A few minutes later, Dirk pulled up and I got in. He was fully camo'd from head to toe, and Skeet hopped around anxiously in the bed of the truck. Dirk glanced at me in my shorts. "Nice outfit."

"Thanks. You look pretty, too."

Dirk put the truck in gear and drove, setting his coffee mug in the cup holder. "We'll be hunting pheasant."

Like I knew what a pheasant was. Sure. I knew what a pheasant was. It was a thing with wings that probably had feathers. "Awesome. Want some coffee?"

He nodded, glancing at his almost empty mug. "Sure."

I poured. "I put sugar in it. Hope you don't mind."

He sipped, then drank. "Nope. Pretty good."

"Miss Mae grinds her own beans. Old-fashioned, you know?"

We drove, and I wondered what separated Dirk and me. He was nineteen years old, but he seemed . . . older. Like you would never question what he was doing. I slouched down in my seat. A few minutes later, Dirk smacked his lips: "Good stuff." He shifted in his seat, speeding up a bit. "I hear Ron Jamison's been giving you hassle."

"Who told you that?"

"I got ears."

"Kim."

He nodded. "He's a punk."

"You know him?"

"Yeah. I worked with him out at his uncle's place when I was fifteen. Before I left."

"He would have been like thirteen."

"Fourteen. He's a year behind in school because he's a dumb shit."

"I take it you don't like him."

He shrugged. "Not worth my time. Kim don't like him one bit, though."

"I know."

He shifted in his seat again, letting out a large fart. He grunted.

I cracked a window. "Nice one."

"Damn."

I breathed through my mouth. "Why doesn't Kim like him?"

"Hell if I know, other than there's not much to like in the first place."

I didn't want to talk about it, because just thinking about it made me nervous. "Jerks are a dime a dozen, I guess."

Dirk pulled out another fart.

"Dang, you got 'em this morning." I laughed, waving my hand in front of my face.

He grimaced. "Musta ate something bad."

"Smells like you've got something dead up there."

He smirked. "Just a raccoon I was saving for lunch."

I spun the lid on the thermos. "Want some more? It might settle your stomach. My mom used to say hot liquid settles things."

He shrugged. "Hell, I'm fine. Just a gurgle." He held his mug out and I poured another cup.

Dirk drove on, and we didn't say much until we'd turned off onto a dirt road. Dirk was the kind of feller that didn't say more than was needed to be said, I'd learned, and I was fine with that. Silence was uncomfortable between most people, but he was the type that you didn't feel weird around. We listened to music and got to where we were going, and there were no expectations.

A few minutes later, Dirk set his mug down and pulled over. "All right."

I looked around. The fields looked like every other field we'd passed for the last fifteen minutes. "This is it?"

"Yeah. To the south." He hopped out, and Skeet jumped from the back of the truck, wagging his tail. Dirk scratched him between his ears. I got out and came around the truck. Dirk winced. "Do me a favor, huh? Grab the shotguns from the cab. I gotta take a shit." He reached in the cab and brought out a travel-size packet of tissues.

"You all right?"

He headed off, toward a gully. "Be fine. Just gotta get it out, is all."

As Dirk disappeared into the gully to take a huge dump because of the quadruple dose of laxative I'd put in my thermos, I smiled to myself. Payback is a bitch. This would be an experience he'd remember for a long, long time. Skeet wagged his tail. "That's right, boy. You tell your master that if he wants to tangle with the King, he'd better be ready for some fun."

A few minutes later, Dirk reappeared and shook his head. "Sausage this morning must've been ripe."

"I hate that."

Dirk spent fifteen minutes explaining how we'd hunt and what Skeet would do to flush the birds out of the wheat, warning me three times to keep my barrel up and away from the dog. We'd be walking, and he showed me how to properly hold the shotgun while doing so, warning me twice more about shooting the dog and three times about staying parallel to him and being aware of your partner. Then he excused himself to go take another crap, mumbling about the sausage.

I didn't have the heart to offer him more coffee before we headed across the fields, and as we entered the wheat, excitement coursed through me. Dirk called here and there for Skeet, prodding him in different directions, and five minutes later the dog flushed the first bird, scaring the hell out of me.

I didn't even have a chance to get my gun up. I just stared at this big and beautiful and colorful thing flying up over the wheat. Faster than the clay pigeons we'd shot. Dirk's rifle was up in a flash, and he let go with a shot, missing. He grunted, cracking the breech of the shotgun and reloading the first barrel. "Fast, huh?"

"Yeah."

Dirk shuffled his feet. "Dude, I gotta go. Like I got a water cannon up my ass." With a pained look on his face, he laid his weapon down and hurriedly unbuttoned his camos, squatting where he was.

I turned around, walking off a few yards and chuckling under my breath. "You got them bad, that's for sure," I shouted.

"Holy shit," came the reply, between grunts. "Like a faucet, man."

A few moments later, he was up and tucking the tissue packet in his pocket. He walked a little funny when we started again. I shook my head, laughing. "A little raw?"

He nodded. "You don't know it, man."

Guilt spread through me. Not enough to feel that bad, but enough to muster up some compassion. "Want to head back?"

"Hell, no. I'm fine. Gotta be empty soon."

Ten minutes later, we swung south and Skeet flushed a pair. I got my shotgun up in time, flipped off the safety, and both of our weapons fired at once. A bird fell. Skeet bounded to it, and a few seconds later appeared with a pheasant in his mouth. Dirk praised him. "You go for the left one or the right one?"

"Right," I said excitedly.

"You got it. I went for the left. Nice shot."

I stared at the dead bird, and an uneasy feeling swept through me. "Pretty."

"They are. Taste even better, though."

"You eat them?"

He smiled. "I don't hold with killing things for no reason."

That made me feel better. "I've never killed anything before."

"Sure you have."

"Well, maybe a spider or two and some ants or bees or something."

Dirk smiled. "Every time you put a piece of meat in your mouth, you killed something. Might not a pulled the trigger yourself, but you killed it."

I'd never thought about it that way. "I guess it's just different."

Dirk laughed. "Doing the dirty work yourself is always different. Come on, let's hunt."

So we did. Dirk squatted three more times, and by the time we got back to the truck, he was walking bow-legged. Every time I felt guilty about what I'd done, I remembered my shoulder. Fair is fair, and I smiled when he told me that he'd be damned if there was a drop left in him.

He'd snagged two birds, and I missed every time after the first. That I missed on purpose wasn't exactly public knowledge, but I had fun. And I had to admit I was proud of my first shot. It was hard to do.

By the time Dirk dropped me off, he *was* empty. We'd stopped one more time on the way home, and when he got back in the truck, he finally showed some pain, shaking his head. "Battery acid, man. Pure battery acid."

"I heard Wal-Mart sells buttholes cheap."

He laughed and I went inside, the pheasant I'd shot in my hand. Miss Mae was in the kitchen, and when she saw it, she smiled. "Well, look what the cat dragged in. Get over here."

I walked over to the counter. "How do you cook it?"

"You dress it first." She took a knife from the butcher block and proceeded to show me how to take the feathers off and then gut it. Let me tell you, bird guts stink like all get-out. I almost puked.

Half hour later, Miss Mae had the bird in a baking dish, seasoned and ready to go. She skedaddled me out of the kitchen and told me to clean up, so I did, calling Kim after I got out of the shower. "Hi, Kim. It's Ben."

"Hey. How'd hunting go?"

"Great. I got one."

She giggled. "That's what Dirk said. He stopped by to use the bathroom before he went out to Uncle Morgan's."

"How's he doing?"

"He said he ate something bad."

I laughed. "Never know."

"Was it that bad?"

I busted up, unable to control myself. "He was squatting like every ten minutes."

Silence, then, "Ben . . . don't tell me you . . ."

"I did. Miss Mae has this stuff in the bathroom. Superlaxative to the rescue."

She laughed, then laughed harder. "He's going to kill you. You do know that, right?"

"Worth it. Totally and one hundred percent worth it. His butthole is going to be raw for just about as long as my shoulder was trashed."

She laughed. "You are a bad, bad person."

"Let him know, okay?"

"Ben . . ."

"It's not a joke unless he knows. You've got to tell him."

"Okay."

Later, over a dinner of stuffed pheasant, I decided one thing as I wolfed down the last of the best fowl I'd ever eaten in my life. Bird-hunting wasn't all that bad.

CHAPTER 21

"I'm going to find her."

Kim looked at me. "How?"

I'd been thinking about Billy since our last conversation, and I couldn't get him out of my head. We sat on Kim's front porch, and there was no moon after a Monday-afternoon scorcher. A breeze rustled the leaves on the maple tree over us. "I've got a buddy in Spokane that's a computer whiz. Like a hacker."

"A hacker, huh?"

"Yeah. He also deals smoke."

"You hung around some interesting people, didn't you?"

I laughed. "I guess."

"How can he help?"

"I don't know, but he'll know. Everybody leaves a trail."

She took my hand. "What if she doesn't want him?"

"That's up to her." Silence folded in around us for a few minutes, and my mind wandered. "Why don't you want me around Ron Jamison?"

She hesitated. "I just don't like him. That's all."

I told her about him following us to the cemetery, then digging up the cats and leaving them on Billy's porch. She shook her head. "Just stay away, Ben."

"Tell me."

She sniffed, then took her hand away from mine. "You really want to know?"

I was sure I didn't. "Yes."

"Ron had a thing for me. For a long time, I guess. When Greg and I dated, he . . . let me know how he felt."

"What happened?"

"Ben . . ."

"Tell me."

She looked at her lap, wringing her hands. "He set the whole thing up. Everything. We went to a party at the Pond one night, and Ron challenged Greg to a drinking contest. Ron won, but he wasn't drunk. He acted like it, but he wasn't. I could tell. He'd fixed it somehow, and Greg was so drunk he couldn't even stand. He blacked out. Ron carried him to the Bronco and piled him in the backseat. I thought . . . I was mad at Ron, and he just laughed it off, saying it was a good practical joke and that Greg would no doubt get back at him somehow. They're cousins, you know? And Ron always did stuff like that to people. I got in the Bronco and told him to take us home, and he did. But he stopped on the way. Greg was passed out. That's when Ron told me he liked me."

My stomach sunk. "He didn't . . ."

"No. He tried, and I fought him. He didn't get what

212

he wanted, and he knew he wouldn't, so he backed off. Then he told me that if I said anything, he'd hurt me." She was starting to cry now. "You should have seen his eyes, Ben. They were crazy. I knew he'd do it."

I put my arm around her shoulders. Threatening to gut the sonofabitch wouldn't make anything better for her right now, so I swallowed my anger. "I'm sorry."

She must have noticed the tone in my voice. She squeezed my knee. "Ben, stay away from him. There's something wrong with him. Seriously wrong. He's done other things, too."

"Like what?"

She sniffed. "I don't know. Just . . . things. It's like he doesn't know when to stop. He just pushes things way too far." She stopped for a moment, then went on. "There's a guy at school named Nathan Tibbs, and Ron didn't like him. I don't even know how it started, but they would go back and forth with each other all the time, you know? Just verbal stuff. Then things started happening. First it was Nathan's car getting keyed. Then somebody dumped bleach in Nathan's gym locker and ruined his baseball uniform. Then Nathan's dog disappeared, and a month later, somebody lit the Tibbses' barn on fire and killed two milk cows and a horse."

"He did all of it?"

She nodded. "Greg told me Ron killed the dog, but I don't know about the rest. The sheriff couldn't prove anything." She looked at me. "The Highway Patrol came in and did an arson investigation. They said whoever did it tied up the animals so they couldn't get out."

"Holy shit."

She folded herself into me. "Promise me, Ben. Promise you'll stay away from him."

For the first time in a long, long time, I lied. "I promise."

Back home, the van was gone and I found Miss Mae in her room. Dad and Edward were probably working on the restaurant. I'd heard something about painting. Miss Mae sat in her favorite rocker, reading. She looked up when I knocked on the doorjamb. "Can't an old woman get a bit of peace around here?"

"No."

She closed her book. "Well, spit it out."

"What do you know about Mrs. Hinks?"

She narrowed her eyes. "Who wants to know?"

"Me."

"You ain't nobody, and it ain't nobody's business."

"Come on, Miss Mae. I just want to know."

"That's a half answer if I've ever heard one. I smell trouble all about you."

"No trouble. At least not with this. I promise."

She eyed me. "Tell me a story and I'll tell you a story."

I sighed. "Okay, I want to find her. For Billy."

She shook her head. "Trouble."

"No trouble. He needs her. Every kid needs a mom, right? You said that when I got here."

"It ain't my business to let on about such things."

I stared at her, my eyes wide. "You know, don't you? She told you!"

"She certainly did. In order to find her if Billy had an emergency or Mr. Hinks died or some such thing of importance. A seventeen-year-old whelp sticking his nose where it don't belong is not such a thing of importance. I still think she's a no-account, but I gave her my word."

I was getting mad, but I knew she was keeping her promise to Mrs. Hinks. "Mr. Hinks abuses him. He does." I told her about the Can. "He puts him in there long enough that Billy doesn't even know how long. He has to pee in a jar."

She frowned. "In a closet?"

"Yes. No light, no nothing."

She stared at me hard, then pointed a crooked finger to her dresser. "Second one on the right."

I slid the drawer open. Ten letters lay stacked in the corner, all addressed to Miss Mae. The sender was Jennifer Lindy. "This is her?"

"Well, it ain't Mickey Mouse. She feared Norman would come after her, but she wanted to keep after Billy. See how he was doing."

I stared at the return address. Las Vegas, Nevada.

Miss Mae spoke up. "She moved some time back. My letters started coming back 'round six months ago, and she hasn't written since."

I studied the envelopes, memorizing the address. "Why'd she leave without him?"

Miss Mae's eyes softened. "Ben, sometimes things happen that don't give a woman many choices."

I nodded. "What happened?"

"Norman Hinks is a hard man. Bitter. Born bitter and will die bitter. Now, mind you, I never saw that man harm his child other than work him hard and strap him every once in a while, but I did see Jenny's bruises."

"He beat her?"

Miss Mae winced. "She's a tough woman, and he came away with a few himself, but when she had to go, she had to go."

"Why didn't she take him, though? Wasn't she afraid that he'd hurt Billy?"

"She was."

"Then why?"

"Because Norman told her that if she ever took his boy, he'd hunt her down and kill both of them. She believed him."

"I'm finding her."

"I know you are."

"You think I'm making a mistake?"

She looked at me. "Why, I don't know. I don't think a boy stuffed in a closet is a good thing, though."

"Well, if she can disappear once, she can do it twice."

"I don't know, Ben. You read those letters and you'll find she has a new husband. Good man, too. He owns a restaurant."

"Can I take these?"

"Return 'em when you're done."

Up in my room, I jumped on the bed. I dialed a number on the cordless. It rang four times, then someone picked up. "Hey, Quaverly," I said.

"Ben? Is this the troubled youth of my past or a manifestation of my imagination?"

Quaverly, besides being my pot supplier, was a computer freak. Illegal computer freak. "You don't have imagination, dude. It's the pot cloud around your head."

"Livin' in the clouds isn't a bad thing, my friend. You back in town?"

"No. I need help, though."

"I don't send through the mail. That's federal stuff."

"I gave up the smoke, Quaverly. Straight as an arrow."

"I was correct, then. The world is coming to an end."

"I need to find somebody."

"Hmmm. Interesting. Care to elaborate?"

I gave him Mrs. Hinks's new name, the city, and the name of the restaurant she gave in the letters to Miss Mae. "I need it quick, too."

Silence on the line for a couple of minutes. I heard fingers on a keyboard. "Okay. Got the info from you, now we'll see."

"Can you do it?"

"As we speak, hombre. Call me back in two hours and I'll have whatever I have."

"Cool. Thanks."

"My displeasure. Now hang up and leave me alone."

After I hung up, I got my jacket on and left, my keys jangling in my hand. When Greg had come over to help with the truck, he'd said he lived on Gordon Lane. I found it without too much trouble, then eased down the street, looking for his Bronco. It was sitting in front of a white one-story house with a small front porch and a Ford F-250 sitting in the driveway. Flowers lined the walk up to the door. I knocked, and a woman with the beginnings of age lines around her eyes answered: "May I help you?"

"Is Greg home?"

She glanced at my truck, then smiled. "Are you Ben? I recognize Miss Mae's truck."

"Yes, ma'am."

"Just a moment." Then she was gone, leaving the door open. A flowery scent drifted from the house, and it reminded me of when my mom had potpourri in our house back in Spokane. Greg came to the door. "Hey, what's up?"

I smiled. "Listen, where does Ron live?"

He frowned. "Over on Hanscomb. Why?"

"Where's that?"

"Take a left on Ellis Street, two blocks down from here, then a right." He paused. "Everything cool?"

"Yeah. Everything settled. He forgot his wallet at the house when we were talking the other day, and I want to give it back to him." I realized how lame that sounded as soon as I said it.

He nodded, not quite sure what was going on. "He's not home."

"Where is he? Miss Mae told me I couldn't come back until I'd given it to him. Something about another person's property or something."

He smiled. "The Pond. There's a party out there again."

"Cool. Where is it?"

"Five miles out on the highway. East. Take a right at Road 2343. Go a mile and you'll see it on the left. There'll be a bunch of cars there." He studied me. "You sure you want to go out there?"

I forced a smile. "Sure. We hashed things out. Just giving the new guy a hard time, you know? He's pretty cool." Silence from Greg, and for cousins, I wondered just how much Greg liked him. "Well, I'd better split. Take it easy, and thanks again for the truck stuff."

"No problem."

I hopped in the truck and drove east on the highway, watching the odometer until I'd gone five miles. A minute later, the headlights flashed against the marker for Road 2343. I took a right and drove down the bumpy dirt lane, looking for cars.

Five minutes later, I came to the spot. I cut the lights early and parked on the side of the road, hopping out and stuffing my keys in my pocket. The Pond was surrounded by brush and spindly pine trees, and as I walked toward it, I heard music. I stopped, circling around to the right, until I saw the glow of a bonfire. I crept through the trees. Twenty or thirty people, the elite of the Rough Butte socialites, sat and stood around the bonfire, listening to country music and partying. A couple of girls danced together in the firelight while the guys hee-hawed and laughed. The Pond was opposite me, a black hole in the moonless night.

It took me a few minutes of creeping around to find

Ron. He sat on a cooler, drinking a beer and slurring his words to a guy in a lawn chair with a straw cowboy hat and Levi's jacket on. I crouched by a tree, watching.

I knew I had to be careful. The thought of twenty or so country boys having a bit of fun with the city kid who was spying on them didn't settle well with me. I broke out in a sweat as Ron threw his empty in the fire, stood, opened the cooler, and grabbed another beer. He opened it and swigged half of it down.

Every few minutes, I noticed the occasional guy head off down a little trail. It took me a while to figure out it was the pee area. I crept closer to it, setting myself in between the party and where a guy was peeing on a log. I could still see Ron through the flickering flames of the bonfire.

Ron drank the rest of his beer and half of another one before he stood up, loudly proclaiming he was going to wiggle the worm. Milk the cow. Choke the chicken. How original. He stumbled around the fire with the beer in his hand, then came down the trail.

I let him pass, and when I heard the splash of liquid falling on leaves, I came up behind him. "Hey, Ron."

He apparently didn't recognize my voice and didn't turn, finishing his business. "Can't a guy even take a leak without . . ."

I came at him from behind, locking my arm around his neck and yanking him to the ground. We landed with a slam, but I kept my grip. "It's me, Ron. Benald. And we need to talk."

He didn't struggle, didn't say a word. Just tried to breathe.

I whispered in his ear: "What would your cousin Greg think if he knew you tried to rape his girlfriend after you tricked him into getting so drunk he passed out?"

Ron held his breath, then exhaled. "You're dead, man. One hundred percent dead."

I tightened my arm around his neck, straining. "No, Ron, I'm not. You don't have the balls to do that. You burn shit down and kill animals and try to rape girls, but you don't face people. You slink around, right? Like the other night when you followed Kim and me to the cemetery." I listened to him struggle to breathe. "Know what's going to happen now, Ron? I'm going to get up and go home and pretend this never happened. You are, too, and you know why?"

He didn't answer.

I jerked my arm around his neck. "You know why?"

"Why?" he croaked.

"Because if you don't, this whole town is going to know what you did. And let me tell you something else. Wanna know what else, Ron?" When he didn't answer, I jerked his neck again.

"What?"

"I don't think Kim's brother would take it very well, do you? Or Greg. Or the sheriff." Silence. I tightened my grip. "Talk to me, Ron. Do you think Dirk would take it very well that you tried to rape his sister?"

"No."

"Good, then, because I'd bet every dollar I have that you'd end up missing if Dirk found out. Just one of those country mysteries, you know?" I paused, waiting for this to sink in. "Now I'm going to let you go, and you're going to get up and grab another beer and think about what might happen if things don't go your way. Got it? Because this didn't happen. None of it did, and you're going to go about your life and I'll go about mine, and everybody will be happy."

He didn't answer, his breathing ragged as I let him go. He lay on his back, staring up at the trees. Then I was gone.

I called Quaverly when I got home. Dad and Edward were putting in another late night at the restaurant. The clock read ten-fifteen. Quaverly picked up. "Hey, Quaverly. Ben."

"Ben-O. Got some news for you."

"Spill."

"They're still in Vegas. New address." He gave it to me, along with a phone number.

"How'd you find out?"

He laughed into the receiver. "If I told you, it wouldn't be magic anymore."

"So be it, buddy. Thanks."

"Drop on by if you're ever in town, huh?"

"Sure thing." I hung up and stared at the phone number, picturing what I'd say to Jennifer Lindy about her son. Nothing worked. *Hey, my name is Ben and I know your son, Billy. He really wants to come live with you.* Or *Hey, your son is being abused by your ex-husband. He makes him pee in a jar when he's living in the closet. Could you come pick him up?*

Nothing seemed right. The phone wasn't right. She'd blow it off. She'd say she was sorry, but that she couldn't do anything. She'd hang up on me. She had a new life. Then I thought about kidnapping the kid and taking him to Vegas. That wouldn't work; this wasn't a movie. Then I decided what I had to do.

I had to tell it to her in person. I had to make her believe.

CHAPTER 22

"I'm going."

Static came over the line as Kim talked. "Ben, you aren't serious. You can't just drive to Las Vegas and ask Billy's mother to come get him."

"Yes, I can."

"Call her. Tell her what's going on."

"You know as well as I that it won't work."

"Ben . . ."

"I have to do this, Kim, and it has to work. He thinks she hates him."

Silence.

"You don't know what it's like to think your mom doesn't love you, Kim."

Silence, then a sigh.

"Come with me."

"What?"

"You heard me. Come with me to Las Vegas. I looked on a map. It's only like thirteen hours if you drive fast."

"I can't. My dad wouldn't let me."

"You can if you don't tell him, but you don't want to come."

"I do want to, but I'm not going to lie."

"Then don't. Leave him a note. Tell him you're not running away, but that you have to perform a civic duty."

She laughed. "I can't, Ben."

"Come with me. We'll be back in two days, tops."

She thought about it. "The only way I could go would be if Dirk came with us. Then my dad would say okay."

I hadn't seen him since hunting. "Is he pissed about the diarrhea thing?"

"He was for a while, but he decided to be a good sport when I reminded him he almost broke your shoulder."

I imagined driving to Nevada with Dirk. "You sure that's the only way?"

A smile lit her voice. "Yes. He does anything I want him to."

"Okay. Fine by me, but we're leaving in an hour."

An hour later, Dirk pulled up in his humongous truck, and he had a humongous frown on his face. Kimberly sat, smiling, in the passenger seat. Dad and Edward were still gone. I hopped in the backseat. "Hey, guys." I leaned forward and pecked Kim on the cheek. "Hey, Dirk. Want some coffee?"

He turned, ready to grab me, but Kim put her hand on his shoulder. "Dirk, you promised."

I smiled. "Come on, Dirk, I nailed you fair and square."

He shook his head, but I saw a smile on his face through the rearview. "Yeah, sure."

I buckled up. "So, how's the ass?"

That got him laughing. He fired the engine up. "You got gas money?"

I nodded. "Gas and food on me. Let's go."

He nodded, in surprisingly good spirits despite chauffeuring us to Las Vegas late night. Kim turned back to me. "What'd you tell your dad?"

"I left a note saying that you were pregnant and that we were going to Vegas to get hitched."

Dirk scowled at me in the rearview mirror. I shook my head. "I'm so joking it's incredible, Dirk. In fact, just knowing you made me sterile." The truth was that I hadn't said a word to anybody.

He drove on. "Tell me the story about this kid," he said.

I did, and as I spoke, I noticed his profile relax. He hit the highway south, and nodded. "He's really screwed up?"

"I don't know. He's just . . . shit, man, I don't know. I guess I owe him."

"You owe him?"

I smiled. "Not really. I just think that if I was him, I'd like somebody giving a shit about me. Besides, I've always wanted to pull a hell run to Vegas."

Dirk cranked it up to eighty on the deserted highway. "You're a different duck, city boy. That's for sure."

I watched the shadowed fields fly by. "You know the way?"

He nodded. "Sure do. Roads the cops don't use, too."

"Cool."

CHAPTER 23

*W*hen I woke up, the dash clock read six in the morning. The landscape flew by. Kim was sound asleep in the front seat, and a slow twang came softly through the speakers. "Hey, Dirk," I whispered. "You tired?"

He spit into the ever-present empty Pepsi can in the cup holder. "You ain't driving this truck."

"Your choice, but I know how to drive, and I just slept."

We drove a couple of miles in silence. Then he let off the gas and pulled over. We were in the middle of nowhere, and I mean *nowhere*. We switched, and he lay down across the backseat. I put the truck in gear. He sighed. "I don't have to tell you what happens if even a bug hits this truck too hard. Go the speed limit."

I didn't smile. "Got it. Speed limit. I'll wake you before we get into the city."

He settled in. "There's a map in the console."

So I drove. I set the cruise at exactly the speed limit, and it was a solid hour before I relaxed even a little bit. I hadn't seen a single car. Kim stirred, then opened her eyes. I smiled. "Hey, Sunshine. Good morning."

She looked at me, then at Dirk sleeping in the backseat. "He let you drive?"

"I'm the dependable type."

She stretched, opening a box of mini donuts and popping one in her mouth. We'd stocked up on junk at a roadside gas station the night before. She chewed, then washed it down with some Gatorade. "You think this will work?"

"I don't know," I whispered. "We'll see."

Hours later, I pulled off to the side of the road and woke Dirk. We were at the Las Vegas city limits, and being that I said I'd wake him when we got there, and also being that I had a suspended Washington State driver's license that everybody had seemed to not ask about, I didn't want to risk getting arrested. I swallowed my guilt. I'd told Dirk I knew how to drive, not that I had a license.

Vegas in the late morning was awesome, and I could only imagine what it would be like at night. Dirk took us through the Strip, and we were able to see all the hotels and casinos. The one that looked like a black pyramid was right up my alley. Dirk drove while I recited the address, and it took us forty-five minutes and a stop at a gas station to find the neighborhood, in a suburb.

We came to a gated entrance to a development called Moran Heights, and luckily the gates stood open. I looked at the houses. I'd expected to find a ho-hum neighborhood, but the only thing ho-hum about this one was nothing. The streets were wide, the gutters clean, and the houses big. "Looks like Mrs. Hinks is doing well," I said.

Dirk searched the house numbers, winding around a corner. We passed a small park with a fountain in it. "Looks like," he said. Then he slowed, pointing. "There it is: 2234."

I looked. These were definitely cookie-cutter houses, probably nine or ten floor plans for the hundreds of houses in the development, but they were nice cookies. Three-car garages, multilevel, small front yards, old-fashioned lampposts strung along the sidewalks—this was yuppie suburbia to the max. A lady with a baby stroller walked down the other side of the street.

I studied the place. "We fit in here like a fart in church." Dirk and Kim laughed. I unbuckled my seat belt. "Do you want to come, Kim?"

She nodded. "Sure."

We walked up the driveway and then to the door, and I heard Dirk cut the engine. Kim took my hand. "Nervous?"

"Me? Naw."

"Liar."

"Okay, a little." Our hands parted as I knocked on the door. We stood there expecting something we didn't know, and after a moment, a lady answered the door. I blinked. Slim and small-featured, she looked young for a mom. Probably thirty or so. And pretty. Her hair was cut short and highlighted with blond streaks, and she wore beige slacks and a light green blouse of some sort. She looked at me, frowning, then looked at Kim. A moment passed. "Kimberly Johan? Is that you? What . . ." Her words trailed away.

Kim stepped forward. "Hello, Mrs. Hinks."

Billy's mother looked at the truck, fear in her eyes. "Mrs. Lindy."

Kim blushed. "I'm sorry."

Mrs. Lindy took a deep breath, then exhaled. "What are you doing here? Are you all right?"

Kim took the lead. "Yes." She introduced me: "This is Ben. He and his dad are living with Miss Mae."

Mrs. Lindy's face fell.

I stuck my hand out. "Nice to meet you, ma'am." She shook it, and just like back home on my bed when I was thinking about what to say, nothing sounded right in my head. I'd thought about it for hours on the way down, but now, nothing came.

A moment of silence passed. Mrs. Lindy's face went slack. "This is about Billy, isn't it?"

I studied her face. "He needs you."

She cleared her throat. "Come in."

Kim and I sat at the dining room table. The house was immaculate. Mrs. Lindy offered us something to drink, and we both declined. She sat across from us. Kimberly smiled at her. "You look different."

Mrs. Lindy nodded. Her eyes pierced mine. "Is he all right?"

I nodded. "He's fine."

A look crossed her face.

"Mr. Hinks doesn't know we're here," I said.

She relaxed, but just a little bit. "I'm afraid I don't understand. . . . Why are you here?"

"He needs you, ma'am. I've gotten to know him since we moved in, and—I don't know. He's a good kid, and he misses you. I guess I just wanted to tell you that."

Her chin quivered for just a moment. "I miss him, too."

"He thinks you don't love him." I looked at her, searching her face. "I guess I came here to find out."

Tears gathered in her eyes. "Of course I do." She dabbed at her face; then both hands went to her stomach. She smiled through her tears: "He's going to have a brother." Then she looked away.

I smiled back, but it wasn't sincere. Anger bubbled up in me, and it was directed at her. Here she was, living in a huge house with her fancy shit in it and wearing her expensive clothes while her son pissed in a jar in a closet. "Cool. Congratulations."

"He's abusing him, isn't he?"

I decided that she deserved the truth—partly to let her know what her son was going through and partly to hurt her. To make her feel like a sorry excuse for a person. I explained the closet and the nonstop work and the strapping, laying down everything I knew, including the cemetery.

By the time I finished, she was staring at her lap, silently weeping, and I wasn't too upset about seeing her this way. A long moment passed, neither of us talking. How could she sleep at night? Then she cleared her throat, wiped her eyes with a finger, and looked around her fine house. "You must think I'm a horrible person for leaving him."

I shrugged. Maybe they didn't have an extra bedroom. "I just came to tell you about your son, ma'am. It's not my business."

She swallowed, keeping her eyes on her lap. Then she straightened her shoulders, nodded to herself, and stood. "Stay here."

Kim and I looked at each other, not saying a word, and a minute later Mrs. Lindy returned. She held a bulging manila envelope. She sat down, putting the envelope on her lap and taking a deep breath. "The last time Norman beat me, he cracked three of my ribs with an iron fireplace poker." She sniffed, her words awkward and stilted. "That night I realized I would end up dead someday. I knew he'd end up killing me. He'd beaten me so many times I couldn't keep count, and I couldn't do it anymore." She cleared her throat. "Billy's bags were packed with mine when his father caught me leaving. He beat me again, told me he'd kill both Billy and me if I ever tried to take him, then beat me some more. Three hours later, at four in the morning, I walked out the front door with nothing, and I never went back."

Tears filled Kim's eyes. "I'm so sorry, Mrs. Lindy, I . . ."

She shook her head. "There's no excuse, Kimberly. Never. I left him with that man. I was twenty-three years old, scared out of my mind, and I didn't know what to do." She paused. "I spent years living on the streets. I hated myself, hated what I did to survive, and I stuck a needle in my arm as often as I could to hide from what I'd done to my son. I thought about him all the time, wondering. I did. But I couldn't go back. I believed with all my heart that Norman would kill him if I did. Kill me."

I looked at her, not understanding. "What happened?"

She smiled through her tears, keeping her eyes down. "I met a woman from an outreach center, and she helped me get clean. It took two years, and in that process I met my husband, Travis, and we cleaned up together." She paused, and a deep kind of pain filled her eyes for a moment. She patted the envelope on her lap. "There's a long story behind what led up to these documents, and it's certainly not your burden." She cleared her throat. "My husband and I have hired an attorney. We've been preparing to get custody of Billy for several months now, and we'll be serving papers on his father soon."

I wanted to melt for her. I wanted to hear the long story behind why it had taken so long to prepare to get custody of Billy, because the pain in those eyes was real. And maybe, I thought bleakly, my own mom felt that way when she talked about me. But another part of me saw only one thing. Excuses.

I remembered one of the things Miss Mae told me when we first met, and I was surprised how true it was. And how much it hurt. "A boy needs a mother," she'd said in the kitchen, and I knew what it felt like to not have one. It was that simple. Cut-and-dried, no bullshit. I looked at her. "I don't think any reason you have matters very much to Billy, Mrs. Lindy. I think he's grown up thinking nobody really cares about him. Especially you."

She swallowed, and tears rushed to her eyes again.

She looked away. "I can't change the past. I can only move forward."

I nodded, knowing it was the mumbo-jumbo crap that counselors vomited when you didn't want to pay your own consequences. My own shrink had told me that. I wanted to lay into her. Flay her alive. She was my dad and my mom all rolled up into one. The victim. The person with a finger pointed somewhere else. "Can I tell you something, Mrs. Lindy?"

She looked at me.

"My mother left me when she found out my dad was gay. I haven't seen her since. Not even a birthday card. She pretends I don't exist."

"I'm sorry. I . . . ," she began.

I cut her off. "I hate her, Mrs. Lindy. I hate her because of what she did. And if you sit there and say you can't change the past, that means I can never love my mother again. And I want to." I paused. "Billy needs to love you. That's all I came to say."

I got up then, without waiting for a response. There was no response. "If you need any kind of testimony or whatever they do, I'll do it," I said.

She sniffed again. "Thank you." She looked at me. "I don't expect anybody to understand why I would leave my son, but I want you to know that I never stopped loving him. I never stopped thinking about him."

I looked back into her eyes, and I saw my mom. "He thinks so."

CHAPTER 24

*M*rs. Lindy sent us off with a hundred dollars of guilt money for gas and food. I finally gave in and took it when I realized I was being an ass to her. I was pissed, though, because every time I looked around her nice house and thought about her nice life, a skinny little kid sleeping in a closet barged into my mind.

I knew the trip was sort of a waste. She'd already started things with the custody hearings, and I knew what I'd done hadn't made a difference and wouldn't make a difference on the legal side of things. I hadn't swayed her one way or another. She'd done it herself.

But it wasn't a waste to me. It was worth the shit I'd get from Dad and Edward, and even if Miss Mae strung me from the nearest tree, I'd smile through it. I'd gone because it was the right thing for me to do, and that made all the difference in the world.

Dirk hauled ass home, and as the afternoon slid into evening, Kim fell asleep in the back. Dirk and I talked about Wyoming. He'd left school and gone to work at the ranch, and he loved it. He was saving to buy his own spread, and when he told me how much he made a year managing the place, all expenses paid on top of things, I could see how he would like it. Another two years, he said, and he'd have enough to buy a thousand acres somewhere and start his own business.

After pulling off at a rest stop to catch some sleep before blasting our way back to Rough Butte, we drove up in front of my house in the middle of the afternoon. Dad was sitting on the front porch with Edward. I said goodbye to Kim and Dirk, then headed up the walk. Neither said a word. I topped the steps. "Hi."

Dad looked at me. "Pack your things."

I stopped, stunned. "What?"

"I said, pack your things."

"Am I going somewhere?"

He swallowed. "Yes. I called your mother, and she's agreed to take you."

I winced. "I'm not living with her."

"Then you'll be on the street, Ben, because you're not living here anymore."

"Why? Because I went to Las Vegas to find Billy's mom?"

He blinked, but let my comment pass. "No. Because you don't have a shred of respect for anybody here, and you don't seem to understand that being an adult doesn't mean walking all over the people who love you. You might think you're a man and that you can do whatever you want, but you're not. You're a seventeen-year-old boy who enjoys hurting people, and I'm done with it."

I clenched my teeth. "You told me to deal with it, so I am. Maybe you should do the same."

He nodded. "I am. Pack your things."

"No."

Edward interrupted: "Ben . . ."

"No. What is this? Another lesson for Ben? Gonna give it to me straight, Dad?"

He leveled his eyes at me. "You are not living here anymore."

I shrugged. "Call the sheriff, then. Have him take me." I pointed to the phone sitting on the table between them. "Pick it up. Call."

"Why are you doing this, Ben?"

"What am I doing, Dad? Huh? You blew me off when we got in that fight, then didn't say a word to me for days, then called me a liar about the cats. And I don't care if you got into a fight with that bastard over it, because it's not like I haven't had my ass kicked because of you."

"Tell me one reason why I should have thought you didn't do it."

"Because I didn't! And I told you I didn't!"

He shook his head. "I don't see that as a reason for you to worry Edward and me out of our minds for the last two days. If you want to be spiteful, you can go somewhere else."

I stared at him. "Oh, it's called 'spite'? I thought doing whatever you want without regard for your family was called 'coming out.' I guess it's different for me?"

He set his chin. "Go."

"You're really doing this, aren't you?"

"No, Ben, you're doing this."

"Fine. Then I am." I slammed the door shut on my way in, then stomped up the stairs to my room, thrashing

237

around for my bags. He could go to hell. He could threaten me all he wanted and it wouldn't work. If he wanted to throw down, we'd throw down.

"Are you done being embarrassed yet?"

I turned, and Edward was standing there. I stuffed a shirt in my bag. "Why would I be embarrassed, huh?"

"Because you're acting like a foolish spoiled brat, and you should be embarrassed."

"Great. Anything else to add?"

He ticked off the items with his fingers, looking up at the ceiling: "Let's see. Selfish, immature, irresponsible, rebellious, mean, and angry. I probably missed some, but those jump out at me."

"Yeah, sure. And he's the angel."

"No, he's not. Neither of you are. I would call it being human."

"What do you want me to do, then? He kicked me out."

"Maybe you should apologize."

I smirked. "You're not allowed to apologize in this house, remember? You get hit with a spoon."

He shook his head. "Maybe you didn't understand her, Ben. She wasn't saying that you should never apologize, she was saying that you should never act in a way that would demand it. There's a big difference there, and honestly, if you walk out that door, it'll be because you let it happen, not because your father made it happen."

I slumped on the floor, deflated. "I tried, man. I took care of Mr. Hinks, I put the antlers back up, I went to Las Vegas to get Billy's mom back, and nothing is good enough. Don't you see it? I can't do anything right, Edward. It's like my life is cursed."

"Like a voodoo curse?"

"I'm serious."

"So am I."

"That's stupid."

He smiled. "Bingo. In fact, it may be as stupid as you two going in circles about it."

"Dead-end road, man. That's all I see."

"You love him, and he loves you."

"Cut it with the Barney routine, Edward."

"Nothing wrong with purple dinosaurs."

I shook my head. "I'm not going to grovel."

He turned. "Then don't."

Miss Mae made herself scarce, and Edward sat reading a *GQ* magazine on the sofa when I finally came down. Without my bags. "Where's Dad?"

I thought I saw an almost imperceptible smile cross Edward's face. He kept reading. "He needed to get out. Try the restaurant."

"Am I still kicked out?"

"I don't know. Maybe you should ask him."

Tired of the whole "maybe you should ask him" gig, I hopped in my truck and drove, resisting the urge to light a cigarette. I figured if I could spend thirty hours riding in a truck with no smoking, I could quit. Dad's minivan was parked in one of the slots in front of the building. "BENJAMIN'S," in fancy script, lit the front of the place. It didn't make me feel good.

Edward and Dad had taped butcher paper over the windows to hide the renovations they were doing, but light came through the cracks and I knew Dad was in there. I got out of the truck and stood on the sidewalk, looking at the place.

Nobody stirred in the streets, and with all the stores closed and the park across the street dark, an aloneness came over me. I wasn't even mad anymore. I was just done. Finished. I knew Dad was right about respect and all that, but it seemed hollow coming from his lips.

This wasn't about the gay thing. This was about him doling out destruction and expecting everybody around him to deal with it the way he wanted. I realized that me standing in front of these doors had been a long time coming, and now, as I stood there, I had no idea what to do.

He'd ruined my life, and as I stood on the sidewalk, looking at the sign with my name on it, I realized that my mother wasn't the one who had left. The second he'd said "I'm gay," he'd been the one to leave. *Let the chips fall where they may. I am who I am.* I hadn't set this up, he had. He'd screwed our lives up, and once Mom was gone, he'd spent three years fobbing me off on other people and expecting them to fix our problems. Now I was out the door.

I remembered telling Billy why people ran. I thought about his mom and the judgment I'd put on her. My dad had spent forever running from who he was, and by the time he stopped running and blew my life up in my face, I realized I didn't know what else my mom could have done.

I stared at the sign and wondered if, before he'd come out of the closet, he figured Mom would take me. If he figured he'd be free to live the life he'd known he was meant for. I thought so. See the kid every other weekend, take him out to dinner, buy him a new skateboard. Put away the boyfriend for a couple of days while good boy Ben was around. I shook my head. Who had abandoned who?

I studied the sign for a minute longer, then got back in my truck and drove home. Miss Mae was asleep, and I didn't talk to Edward, just grabbed my stuff, snagged a blanket from the hall closet, and walked out.

CHAPTER 25

*A*s I hunkered down in the bench seat of my pickup, parked who knows where on the side of some dirt road in the middle of Eastern Montana, I tried to imagine Dad and Edward at home. *He's really gone? He left?*

I didn't know, though. Half of me thought this was some kind of lesson for him to teach me and it pissed me off, but the other half said this was for keeps. No turning back. I was on my own. That feeling sunk into my chest, and I fell asleep with it nagging me.

I woke up to that happy-go-lucky sun damning my eyeballs and a not-so-happy sheriff tapping his nightstick on my window. I squinted, groaning. There were like eighty thousand miles of dirt roads around here, and it was just my luck. I rolled down the window. "Hi."

Sheriff Wilkins eyed me, then studied the cab. "You okay, son?"

"Yeah. Fine."

He nodded. "Got a call from George Tyler about an hour ago saying there was a broke-down truck on his road."

I shook my head. "Not broken-down."

"Something going on?"

"My dad kicked me out of the house."

"Gotcha." He paused, scratching his ear. "Plannin' on going back?"

"I don't know."

He tilted his hat back on his head. "Things happen, I suppose."

"Yeah."

"Tell you what, huh? You come on by the jail at around eight tonight and I'll set you up with a cot. You can sleep there until things are ironed out with your dad."

"In a cell?"

He smiled, then laughed. "Other than Keith Donner getting drunk every once in a while and causing a ruckus with his brothers, I don't think I've had anybody in there for three years."

"Thanks. I'll think about it."

He nodded. "I lock up at around eight."

"I'll remember that."

He tipped his hat. "Keep your chin up, huh?" Then he walked back to his truck and drove away.

After taking a leak and stretching, I drove into town, parking in front of the Cascade Café for some breakfast. Milton Treadway owned the place, and I'd met him once when he was sweeping the walk in front of his door. I'd been skating by, and he told me to mind not knocking him down and breaking his hip.

The Cascade was where all the old-timers met every morning over coffee, and it was in full swing. I took a seat at the bar and Milton took my order, his craggy and wrinkled face almost hiding a set of bright eyes. He looked at me, taking in the John Deere cap on my head and the work boots on my feet, and smiled. "Look a mite different than the last time I seen you."

I smiled. "Smells good in here."

He gave a gravelly laugh. "Might be the only place in town for breakfast, but it's the best." Then he was back at the griddle, cooking up orders.

A few minutes later, he plopped down a huge plate of biscuits, sausage gravy, and two eggs done over easy. All the orders had been cooked for the time being, and Milton leaned his elbow on the counter, eyeing me. "I hear yer daddy's opening a rest-o-ront down the street."

I nodded, sopping up gravy with a chunk of biscuit. "Yeah."

"Hear it's going to be a fancy steakhouse-type thing. Like you might find in the city."

"Yep."

He wiped the counter. "Can't say I wouldn't like to have myself a good steak every once in a while that I don't cook. All the trimmings and such. The wife just might like that, too. Womenfolk like gettin' taken out, you know. All fancied up and such."

I finished up. "Yeah. I heard Edward say it won't be too expensive, either. Big steaks."

Milton took my plate. "Might just be a good thing around here."

I left then, leaving six bucks on the counter, and drove home. I parked at the curb, hopped out, went to the shed, and got my tool belt. Ten minutes later, Miss Mae came outside. She nodded. "Good boy."

I stopped working on the fence. "Miss Mae?"

"Yes?"

"I'm going to have to get a job that pays more."

"Figured on that."

"If I still pay you for the truck, can I keep it?"

She nodded. "That will do." Then she trudged inside, leaving me to the fence.

A few minutes later, Dad walked out the back door and across the lawn. I kept working. He stood there for a moment. "I thought you moved out."

"If that's what you call it, fine." I nailed a board. "I had a deal with Miss Mae."

"Where are you staying?"

I turned. "I guess that's not your problem now, is it?" Then I bent to another board, tacking it up. Dad stood there for a long moment, then turned and walked away.

I finished the fence by four, then walked down to Kim's. Mrs. Johan answered the door. She smiled. "Hello, Ben. Kim has been trying to reach you."

"I've been busy. Is she here?"

She shook her head. "She's out at her aunt and uncle's, helping can peaches."

I thanked her, then drove out to Kim's uncle's place. Dirk's and Kim's trucks were in front of the house, and Uncle Morgan, still in casts, sat on the front porch. He smiled. "Well, if it isn't the feller who saved my hide. How goes it, son?"

"Fine, thanks." I looked at his casts. "How are you?"

"On the mend. Doc says I'll be eighty percent by next spring. That damned tractor had it out for me."

I looked around for Dirk, then thought about something. "Are you hiring?"

He studied me. "Looking?"

"Yessir. I'll do anything."

He smiled. "Kim was a mite upset this morning. Said she called your place and it turns out you and your daddy had a falling-out?"

"Yes."

He nodded. "Got room and board in the bunkhouse, three squares a day, and twelve hundred a month if you'd be interested."

"I don't want this because I helped you."

His eyes twinkled. "Come winter, Dirk's gotta head back to Wyoming and I'll be hiring out anyway. He can teach you the farm until then, but if you see it as charity, I can respect that."

I thought about school starting in a bit, but feeding myself was more important at this point. "You were going to hire out anyway?"

"Sure was. Hard to find good hands, and I'd be happy to pay for Dirk showing you the ropes."

"Then I'll take it."

He nodded, rolling a cigarette. "Start tomorrow if you've a mind."

"I have to finish up a couple of things for Miss Mae tomorrow. How about day after tomorrow?"

"Deal. We got the town potluck tomorrow at four anyway." He smiled. "They're gonna have to wheel me around in a damned wheelchair, but I ain't missed it going on thirty years and I ain't about to miss it now."

I'd forgotten about the potluck. "Okay."

He flipped his thumb to the barn. "Expect you came to see a girl. She's in the barn."

Kim was hanging tack on a hook when I entered. I kissed her, and we sat on a bale of hay. She smelled like peaches. "Are you okay?"

"Yeah. I'm fine. Your uncle just hired me, and I think it'll be good. About time I did something, anyway."

She squeezed my hand, smiling. "It's hard work."

"I can do it."

"I know you can." She looked down, studying the hay-strewn floor. Something small, probably a mouse, rustled between the hay bales. "What about your dad?"

"I don't know."

"I think you should try and make things better."

I took my hand from hers. Shadows fell long in the barn, and its musty smell in the early evening soothed me. "Maybe the best thing I can do is make things better with myself first. Besides, he's done with me. At least for now."

"What if it's too late by then?"

I looked at her. "I don't know, Kim. Half the time I feel like a little kid around him and the other half I just want to hit him in the face. Nothing is ever right, you know?" I stood and paced up and down. "I don't know. I just don't want to be around him. There's too much shit between us, and all the little things just seem to get bigger every time something happens."

"I'm sorry."

"For what? That he decided to have a family when he knew he shouldn't have?"

"No, I'm sorry you two can't get past it."

I rubbed my temples, done thinking about it. My head pounded. "Are we still going to the potluck tomorrow?"

She nodded. "We're bringing a bunch of stuff. My mom's teriyaki meatballs are awesome."

"Cool. I'll pick you up?"

She shook her head. "I'm going with my mom to help set things up. Meet me?"

"Four?"

"Sure." She looked at me. "You could stay in the bunkhouse tonight, you know."

"Naw. I'm fine. Besides, I'm not starting work until Saturday."

"Where are you staying, then?"

I smiled. "Your bed?"

"Ha-ha. Be serious."

"I'll be fine." I kissed her, and I realized right then that something was happening between us. I was falling in love with Kimberly Johan. The kind of love that said I wanted to be with her more than anybody else. "You should get back in and help your aunt."

"Ben . . ."

I smiled. "I'm fine. You forget that I'm a city kid. I spent half my life on the streets."

She rolled her eyes. "Yeah, right."

I ate dinner at the Cascade a couple of hours later, and as I drove by Dad's restaurant afterward, I saw the minivan in front of it. Edward and Dad, especially Dad, had been putting in long hours. I slowed as I passed, trying to catch a peek through the blocked windows, then pulled up to the sheriff's office down the street.

I hopped out of the truck and walked in, and the place looked almost exactly like the jail on *The Dukes of*

Hazzard. Three cells; a couple of desks, one with a mini-TV on it; a locked cabinet full of rifles and shotguns; calendars on the wall; a clock; and a coffeepot. Oh, yeah—and the sheriff sitting at one of the desks, filling out paperwork.

He looked up. "Hello, Ben."

I set my bag down. "Hi."

He stood, walking to the first cell. "Not exactly a Holiday Inn, but it should do."

"No problem. Thanks for the offer."

He put his jacket on, grabbing his keys. "Coffee is in the cabinet below the pot. Help yourself if you've a mind."

I looked at him. "Why are you doing this?"

He put his cowboy hat on, smiling. "When I was thirteen years old, way back when, my older brother took me on a road trip across the United States. He was around your age, had a '37 Buick, and the damn thing broke down every five hundred miles to the mark. Anyway, one time we were stuck in some Podunk Alabama town, freezing our asses off in the middle of the night. Nowhere to stay, nowhere to go. Sheriff comes up and checks us out, right? Hell, we thought he was going to arrest us for loitering. Instead, he did the same for us as I'm doing for you." He opened the door. "Suppose it's a tradition with me."

"Cool. Thanks."

He nodded, tipping his hat to me and smiling. "Might want to get that suspended license taken care of before you get in more trouble than you can afford." He looked at me for a moment, seeing the dread in my eyes, then chuckled. "We might bend a few of the laws we have around here for the sake of practicality, but I can't ignore everything." Then he was gone.

I took my boots off and tucked my socks into them, lying down and wondering how a cop could be so not cop-like. I always thought my dad would have been a perfect cop. He lived by the book, followed the rules, and was totally uptight, just like every cop who'd chased me, cuffed me, or treated me like dirt, but the sheriff wasn't that way. He knew about my license, he was letting me stay here, and for a moment—just a brief instant—I thought that it might be cool to be the sheriff in Rough Butte.

Quickly banishing the sinful thought of Ben Campbell, lawman, from my mind, I padded to the desk to see if the little television got reception. As I did, my eye caught the cabinet next to it. Files. I went to the front door and checked that it was locked, then went back.

Back in his halcyon days of criminality, Ben Campbell had learned one thing well, and that was picking locks. After a couple of minutes with two paper clips and a wiggle-waggle or two, I pulled the cabinet door open. Bingo.

I slid over the files until my fingers came across the *H* section. *Hellerman, Hempton, Hill, Hinks.* Hinks, Norman J. I pulled the file out, whistling as I opened it. Norman had a record. Quite a record for a man of the cloth. I read it and learned that it had started when he was twelve years old and went on up. I counted: he'd been arrested eight times. Defacement of public property, shoplifting, malicious mischief, public intoxication, two counts of assault on different occasions, and three counts of domestic battery. I thought of Mrs. Lindy, then back-tracked to the assault charges.

The first one blew me away: COMPLAINANT: ED-WARD INGERSON. I read further. Edward had been fourteen then, Norman sixteen. Two other boys had been involved, and my stomach lurched as I read the notes. He'd been chased into a barn, taunted, and beaten with fence boards by the three older boys. The sheriff at that time, a man named Logan Vern, noted that the apparent reason had to do with the victim's sexual orientation. Third-degree assault charges had been filed, only to be dismissed by the judge, who cited "boyhood rambunc-tiousness" as the cause.

Reading the notes left in the Norman Hinks file from each of three sheriffs over the years, their handwriting different but still scrawled, I noticed none of them had kind words for the man. *You reap what you sow, you ass-hole,* I thought.

After reading his file, I put it back and stopped, eye-ing the next three files. Then the fourth: *INGERSON, EDWARD.* My eyes widened. Our Edward has a criminal record? I gently lifted the file from the cabinet, still queasy from imagining a fourteen-year-old Edward, ter-rified in that barn.

I opened the file, and was relieved. One charge. The year he moved to Spokane. Possession of an illegal sub-stance. Marijuana. I smiled. Good old Ed and I had something in common, and I didn't blame him at all. I'd have been baked out of my head all the time if I'd lived here as a gay kid.

I put the file back, smiling at the thought of Edward

lighting up a fatty in the fields, and hit the *J* section. There, two inches deep, was Ron Jamison's file. I smiled. "Know thine enemy," somebody had once said. I flipped it open.

As I read the sheriff's scrawl on Ron's file, I realized it was nothing I hadn't heard. Suspicion of vandalism. Shoplifting. Defacing public property. Arson charges brought by the sheriff, then dropped by the district attorney for lack of evidence. Information on the Montana Highway Patrol arson investigation, complete with the fire marshal's conclusion, was tucked inside. Then I turned to the last page. Two papers stapled together and marked *"Confidential"* confronted me.

It was a psychological analysis done by a doctor employed by the Montana Highway Patrol. I whistled as I scanned through the mumbo jumbo. Passive-aggressive nature, leanings toward obsessive behavior. Subject lacks empathy for others. Egocentric. Sociopathic tendencies, with a conclusion by the doctor that symptoms would deepen as the subject reached maturity. Shit. Ron Jamison was one fucked-up cowboy.

CHAPTER 26

I woke to the sound of keys in the door, and as I opened my eyes, Sheriff Wilkins walked in, carrying a mug of coffee and a sack lunch. He nodded, setting the mug down and stuffing his lunch in the small fridge near the coffeepot. "Sleep well?"

I stretched, wiping the gunk from my eyes. "Yeah. Better than freezing in my truck."

He laughed. "Hungry?"

I shook my head. "I'm fine, thanks."

"I'll spring for breakfast at the Cascade if you've a mind."

I laced my boots. I *was* hungry. "I've got money."

He smiled. "Sure. Come on, then."

At five in the morning, the Cascade was just opening its eyes and only a few old-timers sat at a table near the front windows. Sheriff Wilkins nodded as we walked in, saying hello to each as he made his way to the counter and took a seat on a stool. I sat next to him. Milton came from the storage room, wiping his hands with a towel. "Morning, Sheriff."

"Morning."

Milton nodded to me. "Looks like I got a regular here."

Sheriff Wilkins smiled. "Can't let these ruffians run free, Milt. Terror of the town."

Milton laughed, looking at me. "I hear Morgan Johan has a new hand out at his place."

I nodded. "I start tomorrow."

"He's a good man. You done well with helpin' him out of that mess with the tractor."

I didn't have anything to say about that, so I nodded, then read the menu. Milton turned to the grill. "Regular for you, Sheriff?"

"Sure."

Milton grabbed two eggs, cracking them over the grill. "And you, boy?"

"I'll have the French toast, thanks."

As Milton cooked, he and the sheriff talked—small things about the town, the potluck later in the afternoon, the teenagers partying out at the Pond. I listened until Milton slid two plates in front of us and started another order; then we dug in. Sheriff Wilkins dumped catsup on his eggs. "The Johan place, huh?"

"Yeah. Dirk is heading back to Wyoming in a while."

"You think about school?"

I shrugged. "I need money."

He nodded. "Fair enough. You know, though, they got a deal around here for kids need to work their places. Sort of like a homeschool-type thing. Give you a curriculum that you do at night. Good for a diploma, if you're after one."

"I'll think about it."

He sipped his coffee. "You do that." We ate in silence for a while as customers straggled in. Everybody knew everybody, and I liked that. A few even said hello to me, referring to me as "the kid who helped Morgan." Sheriff Wilkins soaked up the last of his eggs with a slice of toast. "Had me a little talk with the young man we spoke of the other day," he said. "I asked him how you two were getting along, and he told me you'd hashed things out and things were smooth sailing."

I grunted, remembering the scene at the Pond.

"Seems you told him you slashed the tires and left those cats. To get back at Mr. Hinks."

"I didn't do it."

"I don't think I said you did."

Silence.

Sheriff Wilkins slid his plate forward, done with his meal. "He's a sly one."

I thought about the file. "Yeah. I've heard."

"See, the funny thing is that whoever did it, they left the knife in the last tire."

"Huh."

"He let me know that in the course of his conversation with you, you said it was the one you had in your tool belt. Left as a reminder to Mr. Hinks that he shouldn't cross you anymore."

My stomach sunk.

He put some money on the counter, then stood. "You keep that tool belt in Miss Mae's shed?"

"Yes. On a hook."

He sighed. "I'd bet anybody could go into that shed and take it if they had a mind to."

"Maybe."

He nodded. "I'm runnin' on a bit of faith, here, Ben. Don't prove me wrong."

"I won't."

"Steer clear of that boy, you hear?"

Too late, I thought, hoping I'd scared Ron enough at the Pond so that he would let it drop. I started doubting it, though, and I wondered how far he'd go. "Sure."

Then the sheriff was gone, saying goodbye to Milton and heading out the door.

When I walked out to the sidewalk, a stage was being set up in the park in anticipation of the potluck later. I'd heard several guys in the Cascade talking about a couple of country bands that would be playing that night, and they said there would be an auction to benefit Morgan's place before the bands took the stage.

I hopped in my truck and drove home. I had to finish up a few odds and ends with the fence, then weatherproof it with stain. I'd seen the minivan at the restaurant and was relieved Dad and Edward weren't at the house. My mind was on Ron Jamison, and my mood was dark because of it. I had a bad feeling about the whole thing, and wondered if I'd made a mistake in how I'd handled the situation.

I thought about the Tibbses' barn. If Ron was the one who'd set it on fire, he had purposely burned the animals to death. To me, that didn't mean regular retribution or vengeance. It meant psycho. Ron Jamison knew no bounds, and the file I'd read had told me just that. I was in trouble.

As I brought the stain from the shed to the fence, I glanced at my tool belt. The knife was gone. No great surprise there. Ron had come in and taken it. He had it out for me, just like he'd had it out for Nathan Tibbs.

Then it clicked.

I set the stain down and walked inside. Miss Mae was nowhere to be found, and I heard the water running upstairs as I reached for the phone and dialed. "Hello, Kim?"

"Hi, Ben."

"Busy?"

"Cooking with Mom. Everything all right?"

"Yeah." I explained that I'd spent the night at the sheriff's office, and she laughed. I cleared my throat. "Remember when you were telling me about that guy Nathan Tibbs?"

Her tone changed. "Yes."

"Well, I was wondering . . ." I paused. "Did you date Nathan?"

"No."

I sighed in relief. "Cool."

"He had a big crush on me, but we didn't go out."

My relief disappeared. "When?"

"Freshman year. Why?"

I reeled, my mind scattered. Ron had Nathan in his sights two years ago. Their freshman year. "Greg mentioned it. No biggie."

She laughed. "Scoping out the competition again? I swear, Ben . . ."

I forced a laugh. "I know. That jealous bone. Never happen again." I paused. "We're still on for the pot-luck, right?"

"Four o'clock."

"Good. Well, I've got to finish up this fence. Happy cooking with Ma."

She laughed. "Bye."

I hung up, my heart pounding in my chest. It was Kim. Ron had some kind of fixation on her, and I was next in line.

I spent the day staining the fence, putting two coats on after Miss Mae came out and barked, "Put two coats on it. Both sides, you hear?" It was three-thirty by the time I finished, and as I walked to the shed to put the stain away, Dad and Edward pulled into the driveway. Edward called hello and walked inside, but Dad came my way. He looked at the fence. "It looks good."

"Thanks." I set the can on a shelf.

Dad shifted on his feet. "So, how are you?"

I looked at him. "I'm fine."

"The sheriff stopped by the restaurant today."

"Somehow that doesn't surprise me."

"He told me what he thinks is going on."

I shrugged.

"I shouldn't have doubted your word."

I frowned, shaking my head. "I probably would have thought the same thing."

He looked around, uncomfortable. "He told me you got a job out at Morgan Johan's place."

"Yeah. I start tomorrow." I hitched a thumb to the fence. "I wanted to get this done first."

Dad cleared his throat, exhaling. "Wow."

"What?"

"I don't know, Ben. I just didn't think it would happen this way."

"Didn't think what would happen this way?"

"Everything, I suppose."

I smiled. "You kicked me out."

"Yes, I did."

I stuffed my hands in my pockets. "Maybe it was the best thing."

"You'll be staying at Morgan's?"

"Yeah."

He nodded. "What about school?"

"I can do homeschooling stuff. The sheriff told me about it."

"You're going to?"

"I think so."

"Good."

"Yeah, I think so, too. Good."

"You know, if things don't work out at Morgan's, you can come back."

"Thanks."

He nodded. "Well, anyway, Edward and I were wondering if you'd like to come by for dinner tomorrow night. Maybe invite Kim if that would be better."

I thought about it. "I'd like that."

He walked up the porch steps. "Hey, Ben?"

"Yeah?"

His eyes met mine. "I'm proud of you." Then he opened the door and went inside.

I stared at the old cans of paint and stain on the shelves, and for some reason, tears filled my eyes. I wiped my face on my sleeve. We'd just had a conversation that was different from any other we'd ever had. Not good and not bad, but . . . different. And, I thought as I focused on the newer can I'd just put away, maybe different forever.

CHAPTER 27

$\mathcal{B}$y the time I got out of the shower, it was ten after four and I was late. Miss Mae, Dad, and Edward were already gone, having lugged four trays of her famous Miss Mae's Montana Corn Bread to the car, and the house was silent as I got dressed. My mood lightened after talking with Dad, and I knew things were getting better. I would be a guest at their house for dinner, and that was weird, but I kind of liked it. Maybe we could start anew. I hoped we could.

On my own. I smiled at that idea. I'd never even given a thought to Ben being a grown-up big boy before, and now I liked the idea. I'd had friends that had moved out before they graduated school, and I would be eighteen in four months, so it wasn't like I was on the streets. Besides, Rough Butte only had one street, I thought with a chuckle. I had a job, a truck, a place to stay, and I'd get my diploma. Not bad.

As I hit the front door and stepped onto the porch, I heard the crash of breaking glass and looked over at the Hinkses' house, an instant pang of guilt shooting through me. In all my planning, I'd almost forgotten Billy, and I felt like a jerk for it.

Billy stood in the driveway, looking at the shattered remnants of a casserole dish, its creamy tuna-and-pasta contents an oozing pile on the cement. He stared at it, then bent, trying in vain to scoop it up. I groaned.

Mr. Hinks came to the door at the sound of the crash and, seeing Billy kneeling on the driveway with tuna casserole all over his hands, came out and walked down the porch steps. He strode across the driveway with his jaw clenched and his hands balled into fists. "Dammit, Billy! Lookit what you've gone and done now." He growled as he reached Billy, then swung his fist, knocking him on the side of the head and sending him sprawling on the driveway. Mr. Hinks stared at the mess. "Told you once, I told you a million times—you gotta be careful when I tell you to be careful! Dammit!" Then he turned on Billy. "I told you to be careful, didn't I?"

Billy rubbed his head, staring up at his father.

"Didn't I? Answer me, boy!"

"Yessir."

Mr. Hinks shook his head, disgusted, then mumbled under his breath as he stared at the broken glass. "Worthless piece of shit can't even take a damn dish to the car." Then he turned and barked, "Get on inside!"

Billy stood up, shifting back and forth on his feet. "What about the potluck? We can still go. I'll clean it up. I promise."

"You ain't going nowhere. Now get yourself in that house before I strap you right where you stand!"

Billy was off, running up the steps and into the house. Then Mr. Hinks noticed me standing there. "What the hell are you looking at?"

"Nothing."

"Then get the hell out of here before I whip your ass, boy. I ain't kidding, either. Get!"

I walked back inside, my heart hammering in my chest. Rage had lit his eyes. I stood in the living room for a moment, not knowing what to do, then peeked out from the shades. Mr. Hinks had picked up the broken shards and was hosing off the driveway, talking and cussing to himself about his worthless son. Then he went inside.

I waited a moment longer, and then heard his screen door slam shut. I peeked again and watched as Mr. Hinks got in his car and drove away, leaving Billy inside. I was already late and knew Kim would be looking for me, so I grabbed my keys and grumbled about what a bastard he was. Billy had been looking forward to the potluck all summer. His mother would have him soon enough, though. That was for sure.

When I got to the park, red, white, and blue streamers fluttered from the lampposts and through the trees, and the whole town gathered and milled around, visiting and eating and drinking beers. At least twenty picnic tables, lined up in a row, held enough food to feed an army, and ice-filled aluminum tubs placed sporadically along the feeding line held bottles and cans of beer. I found Kim watching two kids get their faces painted.

I scanned the crowd for Mr. Hinks as I walked up to Kim. "Hey." I pecked her on the cheek.

"You're late. I was beginning to think you dumped me and moved back to Spokane."

"Nope. I got caught up."

Kim smiled. "Forgiven."

I nodded, taking her hand. "Hungry?"

"Starving."

As we walked through the park, I told her what happened to Billy.

"Well, his mom is going to get him soon," she said.

"I know. It just sucks."

"Yes, it does."

"He's in the Can. I know it." I grabbed two plates and we meandered down the food line, picking up this and that and filling our plates. I was sure to load up on Mrs. Johan's teriyaki meatballs, and made sure Kim noticed. I popped one in my mouth. "Mmm. Good."

She laughed. "Brown-noser."

"That's me. Come on." As I led Kim to a tree and we sat under it, the mayor got up onstage and began announcing the schedule of events for the afternoon and evening. The grand finale would be Two Tone Slim and the Taildraggers performing some toe-tapping, knee-slapping, hot-off-the-presses country for everybody. Then he said that he had an announcement to make. He cleared his throat into the microphone. "Now, we all know Morgan Johan up and decided to get himself trapped under a tractor. . . ." Laughter from the crowd. He went on: ". . . and busted himself all up. That's in part why we're here today. As I said, we'll be starting the auction in a few minutes, but first I'd like to have two people come on up on this stage." He paused. "Will Kimberly Johan and Ben Campbell please come on up."

Kim and I gawked at each other. I had three meatballs stuffed in my cheek. "Whuff doesh he whant?"

Kim frowned, then smiled. "I don't know. Come on, though." She took my hand, and we wound our way through the crowd. Once we reached the stage, the mayor had us stand next to him. He spoke into the microphone: "Ladies and gentlemen, these two young adults at my side stand for something we all cherish in Rough Butte. They stand for a willingness to help those in need and the backbone to stand up and make themselves be counted when emergencies arise. They stand for courage and heroism and duty to their neighbors, but most of all, they stand for doing what's right when there's something to be done." With that, Sheriff Wilkins walked onstage with two certificates, handing them to us. I caught sight of Dad, Edward, and Miss Mae. Edward was dabbing his eye, and Miss Mae beamed with pride before she smacked Edward on the shoulder, no doubt telling him to dry up.

I smiled, blushing, and looked over the crowd. That's when I saw Ron Jamison standing at the edge of the park, staring at me. He smiled, then walked in the direction of our house. I stopped breathing, the hair on the back of my neck prickling ominously. The mayor went on: "In honor of Kimberly Johan and Benjamin Campbell going beyond the call of duty in saving Morgan Johan's life, these certificates of community service and bravery are bestowed upon them as a mark of heroism. We thank you from the bottom of our hearts, and . . ."—he smiled—"I'm sure Morgan looks kindly upon it, too."

The crowd erupted with applause, and Edward was openly weeping like the proudest mother in the world. My dad's eyes gleamed. I watched as Ron disappeared around the corner. Then the mayor handed the microphone to Kim, smiling. "A few words?" he said.

Kim took the microphone, staring at the crowd. She hesitated, took my hand, squeezed it, and spoke: "Well, I guess I'm just glad Uncle Morgan is all right, but I didn't do much. It was mostly Ben. He stayed while I got help." Then she handed the microphone to me as the crowd clapped.

I took it, ready to pee my pants. I cleared my throat. It was no use. The Ultimate Ben Campbell would come out and screw things up. I'd say something stupid. That much I knew. "Um . . . thanks. I don't really . . . uh . . . yeah, those teriyaki meatballs sure are good, huh?"

The crowd erupted in laughter and applause, and I saw Mrs. Johan blushing. I handed the microphone back to the mayor, and we left the stage. Dad came up to me, with Edward in tow. Edward had gained control of himself and beamed. Dad held his hand out. "Congratulations, son."

I shook it, and several men I didn't know patted me on the back as they passed. "Thanks," I said.

Dad smiled. "You've done well, Ben."

I nodded, smiling back. "I guess I learned it from you, huh?"

Dad's face almost crumpled, and Edward was all

over the place with the tears again. Dad hugged me then and, lowering his voice, spoke into my ear: "I love you."

I hugged him back. "Love you, too."

Kim and I glad-handed for the next few minutes, but I was anxious. Finally, when we'd made our way through the crowd, and when the auctioneer, who happened to be Mr. Hinks, kicked off the action with spitfire bidding going on over a saddle donated by Gunderson's Hardware, I tucked the certificate in my back pocket. I looked at Kim, thinking about Billy. "I've got to take a leak. I'll be back," I said.

She shook her head, smiling. "Too much information. I'll be at the tree."

I kissed her, then looked into her eyes. "You know, I could end up loving somebody like you. Since we're both heroes and all."

She laughed. "Slow down, hero. Go pee, and then we'll talk about love."

I left then, but I didn't go to the bathroom.

CHAPTER 28

I ran. My breath came in ragged heaves and my chest felt like it would explode, and when I finally got to Mr. Hinks's house, I stopped. No sign of Ron. I walked across the lawn, looking, but he was nowhere to be found. My heart slowed. Maybe I'd been wrong. I walked up the Hinkses' drive, then across our side yard to the back.

"I knew you'd come."

I turned, and just before everything went black, I saw Ron Jamison and the two-by-four flashing toward my head.

I woke up coughing. I felt like forty midgets with jackhammers were playing tag in my head. I coughed again. Smoke. I jerked up and felt the heat on my face, my eyes going to the Hinkses' house.

Flames licked the eaves, and I heard the sirens already. I didn't know how long I'd been out, but the house was almost fully engulfed. I stood up, the pain making me dizzy, and looked around. Billy. I searched the grounds. No Billy.

Then I knew. The Can.

I ran.

The front door was on fire, and as I scrambled to the back, flames licked the siding of the house. The sirens grew louder. Smoke billowed in the sky. Two empty gas cans lay scattered on the driveway, and as I reached the door, I saw Ron Jamison standing in the field behind the house, smiling at me. Then he was gone.

I tried the back door, but it was locked. In a panic and with the heat searing me, I kicked three times before the door gave way. Then I was inside, screaming for Billy. No answer.

Flames had spread up the walls and across the ceiling. As I screamed for Billy, the heat sucked into my lungs stopped me from breathing. I choked, running through the kitchen with my shirt over my mouth. Smoke clouded the rooms and I knew I was almost out of time. He'd die. I'd die. Time stopped. I kept running. I opened doors to flames and smoke and heat, and finally, in the hall, I found it.

The Can. I opened the door, and through the smoke I saw Billy huddled in the corner. His eyes were closed. I yanked him up and carried him, my shirt falling from my mouth. I couldn't breathe. My eyes burned and my ears were filled with the dull roar of flames. I ran to the closest room as the hair on my arms curled up and the heat seared me. My entire body ached. Then I found a window. Without a thought, I dropped Billy, braced my hands on the sill, and kicked the glass out, cutting my arms as I frantically cleared the wicked shards.

Arms slick with my blood, I picked up Billy's limp body, the acrid smoke almost smothering me as it poured from the window, and shoved him through. His foot caught on the sill but he tumbled to the grass, then I dove out myself, landing in a heap on top of him.

Cool air. Light. I sucked in a breath, then dragged Billy away, yanking him out of reach of the flames. My head spun. I couldn't get enough air into my lungs. The sirens screeched. The last thing I saw was three men in yellow jackets running toward us.

When I came to, a man's voice was explaining something about smoke inhalation. I heard Dad's voice, and opened my eyes. He and a firefighter stood over me. The Hinkses' house was still burning. I looked over and saw Billy sitting up, his face covered with soot, his father standing yards away, staring at the inferno. My own father's face—his expression, the look in his eyes as he studied me—needed no words, and I realized right then that no matter what happened between us, one thing would never change. He loved his son. And I loved him.

EPILOGUE

*R*on Jamison was charged with arson. Montana is a wild place, but the judge didn't take it too kindly that a little boy was almost killed. He sentenced Ron to juvenile detention, with a transfer of four years in prison when he turned eighteen. He also mandated heavy psychiatric treatment. Ron is appealing the verdict, but I don't care. He's gone, and that's all that matters.

Sheriff Wilkins served Mr. Hinks with custody papers one week after his house burned down. The custody hearing was set for a month later, and by the time I gave a deposition on what kind of treatment I'd seen Mr. Hinks give Billy, my eyebrows and arm hair had grown back. Mr. Hinks lost custody of Billy, and with no home and under threat of arrest by the Montana Highway Patrol and the FBI for promising to get revenge on Mrs. Lindy, he left Rough Butte. No one knows where he lives now.

Mr. Hinks never thanked me for saving his son's life. Billy did, though, and he writes me from Las Vegas every once in a while. They have three cats. Mrs. Lindy calls Miss Mae, too, asking after us. Billy's little brother was born without a hitch, and they named him Christopher and say he's got Billy's eyes.

Billy got a new skateboard for his twelfth birthday, and he tells me he's getting pretty good with it. He's in school, happy, and decided to join the baseball team. Mrs. Lindy sent us a picture of him in his uniform, and I barely recognized him with his hair grown out and a few pounds put on his scarecrow frame. I miss him.

Dad and Edward had the grand opening of Benjamin's, and it got rave reviews from the local paper. Great steaks, friendly service, decent prices, and they're busy. The town seems just fine with them, and I'm glad that I was so incredibly wrong about this place. The people of Rough Butte are good.

Me? Well, this place, this last exit to normal, taught me that nothing is ever really normal. It's what you make it. I got my damn license, I'm working at the Johan place, and Dirk left for Wyoming a while back. I bust ass every day, then study at night. I'm saving to buy a new truck. Morgan Johan is a good man, and he told me I have a job as long as the place is here.

Dirk forgave me for giving him the shits. Skeet sired a litter of puppies, and Dirk gave me one before he left. I named him Moe. I eat supper at Miss Mae's a couple times a week with Dad and Edward, and sometimes Kim, too. Miss Mae is eternal, I think. She'll never die. She did retire the wooden spoon, and she even let me hug her once.

Dad and I are getting along better, and after several beers one night, Edward finally admitted that he smoked pot as a teenager, and I didn't let on that I already knew. I'll give him a hard time about it forever.

I called my mom, too, and I was scared to do it. Scared of what she'd say or not say, and scared it would all come back to the surface like some festering wound. It didn't. There was pain in her voice, the kind that I knew and understood, even after almost four years, and I realized that she was just as human as I was. We talked for over an hour, she told me she loved me, and she gave me the answer to something I'd wondered about since she left: she had loved my dad, and she still did. That's why leaving him hurt so bad.

She also said that maybe in a while, when she felt ready, she'd come to Rough Butte to visit. I don't think she will, but maybe I'm wrong. Just like Miss Mae told me one time after dinner as she and I sat on the front porch: time is a blessing. We'll see.

Every now and then, when the sun goes down and the moon rises full over that huge and empty sky I hated so much when we got here, I go to Billy's ruined pet cemetery and sit, thinking about everything that led me here. That led us here. All the crap and turmoil that we'd been through and all the things that had almost destroyed me brought us to this place. Who would have known?

And each and every time I sit in the moonlight on the rise overlooking all those dug-up graves, I tell myself I like it here. It fits. I can do something here, and I can be somebody here. I shake my head and laugh every time I think about it. Ben Campbell, country boy. My friends in Spokane wouldn't know me.

And then there's Kimberly Johan. Yeah. Kimberly Johan. I think I'll stay.

ACKNOWLEDGMENTS

*T*hanks to my wife, Kimberly, the strongest woman I know, and to my family. To George Nicholson of Sterling Lord Literistic: thanks and gratitude for the faith, enthusiasm, friendship, and vast experience. Thanks also go to my editor, Joan Slattery, and her assistant editor, Allison Wortche, for advising and working with me in such extraordinary fashion. And, as always, thanks are in order for that timeless place, The River.

ABOUT THE AUTHOR

*M*ichael Harmon is the author of *Skate,* a "remarkable first novel," according to *Kirkus Reviews.* He was born in Los Angeles and now lives with his wife and two children in the Pacific Northwest, where he is at work on his next novel for Knopf. To learn more about Michael Harmon and his books, please visit www.booksbyharmon.com.